FIRST, he showed his thoughtful generosity. Then he shared his risqué humor. Now it's time he declares everything... If only he didn't constantly wrestle with words!

AN EVENING at the opera could prove Lord Tremayne's undoing when he and his lovely new paramour cross paths with his sister and brother-in-law. Introducing one's socially unacceptable strumpet to his stunned family is *never* done. But Daniel does it anyway. And it might just be the best decision he's ever made, for Thea's quickly become much more than a mistress—and it's time he told her so.

Thea's fallen under the enticing spell of her new protector. How could she not when his very presence, every kindness and written word has utterly seduced her senses? Yet her mind insists on knowing more, such as why must Lord Tremayne pummel his face in boxing matches and be so abrupt in person? Curiosity turns to baffled amazement when his sister seeks out Thea, begging advice. If that weren't surprising enough, when circumstances conspire and Thea arrives—unannounced—at his home, she's not only welcomed inside but confronted with more truths than she ever expected.

DARING DECLARATIONS BEGINS DIRECTLY AFTER BOOK 2, *LUSTY LETTERS*.

DARING DECLARATIONS

A STEAMY STUTTER REGENCY

LARISSA LYONS

Daring Declarations is dedicated to the utterly delightful Martinique, whose friendship—and enthusiasm for my stories—mean the world. Your joie de vivre and bright smiles light up every room you enter. If sunshine and glitter (mixed with a dollop of brownie batter) had a name, 'twould be yours.

This series is dedicated to anyone who has difficulty speaking up for themselves. May you find a way to be heard.

Larissa's Complete Booklist

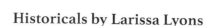

Historicals by Larissa Lyons

ROARING ROGUES REGENCY SHIFTERS
Ensnared by Innocence
Deceived by Desire (2022)
Tamed by Temptation (TBA)

MISTRESS IN THE MAKING series (Complete)
Seductive Silence
Lusty Letters
Daring Declarations

FUN & SEXY REGENCY ROMANCE
Lady Scandal

A SWEETLY SPICY REGENCY
Miss Isabella Thaws a Frosty Lord

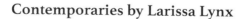

Contemporaries by Larissa Lynx

SEXY CONTEMPORARY ROMANCE
Renegade Kisses
Starlight Seduction

SHORT 'N' SUPER STEAMY
A Heart for Adam...& Rick!
Braving Donovan's
No Guts, No 'Gasms

POWER PLAYERS HOCKEY series
My Two-Stud Stand*
Her Three Studs*
The Stud Takes a Stand (2022)
*Her Hockey Studs - print version

CONTENTS

DARING DECLARATIONS

Daring Declarations begins directly after Book 2, *Lusty Letters*. If you missed either that or Book 1, *Seductive Silence*, here's a *quick* summary:

Pestered by a persistent stammer, a Regency lord takes a new mistress, a refined widow who's as unsure of her seductive allure as she is tired of living in the slums of London. The enigmatic Lord Tremayne sparks her interest even as his perpetual silence befuddles her brain. After several scorching nighttime encounters—the hours between filled with racy correspondence that delights them both—Daniel spoils his enchanting inamorata with thoughtful trinkets, dashing dresses and then, reluctantly, even proposes a night on the town, hoping the excitement will help hide his stammering secrets.

He's also learned Thea has secrets of her own,

ones from her past she'd rather forget but which threaten to snatch the lovely widow from the safety of his arms. And now, amidst angst over a blasted *speaking* engagement, boxing matches where he likes to let his fists talk for him, and agonizing over that broken orrery he dreams of repairing, Daniel escorts his lady lust to the opera...

Then pray speak aloud. It is of all subjects my delight.

— JANE AUSTEN, *PRIDE AND PREJUDICE*

BOTH PLEASURE AND SUFFERING

Voi, che sapete che cosa è amor,
Donne, vedete, s'io l'ho nel cor.
Sento un affetto pien di desir,
Ch'ora è diletto, ch'ora e martir.

You who know what love is,
Ladies, see if I have it in my heart.
I have a feeling full of desire,
That now, is both pleasure and suffering...

Le Nozze di Figaro (The Marriage of Figaro), a popular
opera first performed in 1786

———◦—

THEA WAS AFRAID TO BLINK. *What if she missed
something?*

Bypassing the ticket booth, Lord Tremayne
conferred briefly with an employee before guiding

her straight through the foyer and up one of several sweeping staircases.

Muted music indicated the performance was well underway.

Mayhap arriving late was to their benefit? No one to see her gawking like a chicken. Of a certainty, the large rounded lobby they came out at on the second level was only sparsely populated.

Lord Tremayne paused before entering either of the two opposing corridors that she assumed led to the private boxes, some costing in excess of two thousand pounds per season she'd heard. That was a vast sum more than most people earned in years, abundantly more than she'd ever come across—and she was *here*, as his guest. An occurrence he still seemed less-than-thrilled about.

"You have a box?" She hazarded conversation once again.

Stone-faced, he nodded, then gestured toward refreshments available for a coin.

"Thank you, but no," she told him, far too uncomfortably aware to eat or drink anything. She patted her hair, afraid the feathers might incinerate if his glare became any fiercer. For a man who insisted he *wanted* to be out with her, he seemed remarkably disgruntled. "I'm not thirsty, but if you—"

He grunted and took off toward the right, her light hold on his forearm whisking her down the passageway as effectively as if he'd picked her up and tossed her ahead. Practically skipping to keep up with him, she prayed the figure-filling padding would stay put. The last thing she needed was to leave a trail of dropped cotton marking her every step.

Narrow doors flanked the corridor, spaced every few feet. They passed a dozen or more before he slowed to find the one he sought. Like most, it was closed. He turned the handle and stepped back, gesturing for her to precede him.

After the well-lit hallway, it took her eyes a few seconds to adjust to the darkened interior. In that short time, she was showered with a wealth of impressions.

Smaller than she'd expected, the box itself was a cozy space, extending only a few paces in either direction. From about waist high, it opened out in the front, overlooking not only the massive stage currently occupied by twirling ballerinas—what an unexpected boon!—but the opening also allowed a glimpse into the noisy gallery below and beyond that—

Thea gasped at the magnitude of it all. Why, there had to be five levels of private boxes, all filled with an assortment of gaily dressed people. Branches of candles extended out every few boxes, illuminating some areas better than others, but everywhere her flitting glance landed, a new and dazzling sight met her eyes.

The spinning, jumping ballerinas cavorting across the stage; a full orchestra playing in front; and behind the musicians, the writhing pit of masculine voices and shapes, only half of whose attention was focused on the performers, the others—like Thea—craned their heads to inspect the individuals lining the boxes on either side.

Some of the occupants stood near the openings, gazing raptly at the stage, others conversed, paying no heed to the spectacle they'd come to see, and others...well, more than one box had the curtain pulled for complete privacy and if she wasn't mistaken—it was difficult to be certain, given the distance and amount of smoke the many candles gave off—but across the expanse, in one of the highest boxes, she *thought* she glimpsed a pair of exposed breasts just before they were covered by two broad palms and both bodies disappeared into the shadowed recess—

Thea swallowed hard and quickly returned her attention to the private box *she* was privileged enough to enjoy tonight.

Chairs. There were several. She blinked as they came into focus.

Oh Lord, levitate me right to Lincolnshire! Lord Tremayne had barged into the wrong box—for two of the chairs were occupied.

The impressions of grandeur still brimming in her mind, one thought screamed above the others: *Escape!*

She reversed direction but he'd come up behind her, his hard body preventing retreat. His breath caught audibly as he took notice of their company.

Then everyone spoke at once.

"Tremayne?"

"*Daniel?*"

"Ellie!" burst from the man behind her, the immovable force who curved one hand around the side of her waist with a tense grip that should have hurt—but oddly didn't. "Wylde. What..."

The other man gained his feet, giving the impression of pure, lean elegance. He was immaculately turned out, not a strand of dark blond hair askew. But his lips? Those were definitely off-kilter as he shot her a contemplative look. A single look that conveyed various emotions: curiosity, speculation, censure perhaps?

And she'd thought Lord Tremayne had an intense manner? My, oh my...

Stepping toward them, he said, "Appears we both chose the same night."

When the woman stood and came to his side, Thea tried again to edge around Lord Tremayne. The bite of his fingers stayed the impulse.

What should she do?

The slight blonde fixed her with a decidedly inquisitive stare.

Under ordinary circumstances, Thea was confident she could hold her own. But this was anything but ordinary. Associating with Sarah and Lord Penry and others of the demimonde ilk was one thing. But a man did *not* mingle his mistress with his—

His *what*?

Who were these people to Lord Tremayne? His friends?

Strangling the strings of her reticule so tightly it was a wonder they didn't snap, she gave a fast, modest curtsy to both the lord and his lady (as competently a curtsy as one can make when their waist is shackled). "Pardon us for the interruption," she said since no one else seemed inclined to speak since the initial outbursts. "We'll take ourselves off, let you return to your evening alone. Forgive us."

But though she again pressed into the brick wall that was Lord Tremayne, he refused to waver. And though Thea *knew* they had to leave, the scrutiny on the other couple's faces was growing.

It was as though she dreamed the next few moments when the woman stepped forward, ignoring the indrawn hiss of her companion, to offer a shallow curtsy of her own. Her eyes flicked back and forth between Thea and the man behind her. "Daniel, aren't you going to introduce me?"

"Ellie," Lord Tremayne said again and his breath brushed across the top of Thea's head, sending a wicked shiver racing across her nape.

How could he stand there? Cage her there as well?

They *must* leave! This woman was Quality. Unmistakable breeding shone in her perfect manner, in her exquisitely coiffed hair and extravagant dress, both of which she wore without a speck of the self-consciousness plaguing Thea.

Already, she'd had to stop herself from fiddling with feathers and checking her bountified bosom. Just how secure—

"Mrs-Hur-well."

Thea heard the ragged syllables come from over-head and for a startled second didn't recognize them as her name.

What was he doing?

She spun within his grip, thankful the glossy material allowed the move. "Lord Tremayne," she said through barely moving lips, the words fast and low, "should we not vacate and leave the box to your friends?"

He ignored her. Ignored her words, that was.

Because right there in the dim interior of his box, partitioned off from the adjoining neighbors but fully visible to anyone with exceptional eyesight in the boxes across, he lifted her hand, inclined his head and turned her to face the other couple.

"Thea, Lord Wylde and his wife, my s—"

Good God, man, some remnant of Daniel's conscience railed. *You can't introduce your fancy piece to your sister.* Bloody hell, he couldn't even *acknowledge* her, not in front of a gently bred female.

Gads. What was he thinking?

Losing it, he was. The ability to think. To act. To behave as he ought.

And why in blazes had that sentence flowed like silk when everything else he'd uttered in the last hour faltered forth like dirt-encrusted flies?

The crux of it was he *wanted* the two cherished

females in his life to meet, to get on with each other as well as he—

Cherished? Thea?

Aye, so she was, he could admit to himself, and as she was also tugging on his arm to the point he should fear losing it, he really ought to behave with decorum.

So he tightened his hold on Thea's hand and started backing out. "A-p-pologize. We'll go elsewhere—"

"Wait!" Ellie's raised voice surely raised more than one eyebrow in the vicinity. "Don't go. Not yet."

On the verge of crossing the threshold, Daniel paused. He watched an indecipherable look pass from Ellie to her husband.

Tense seconds later, Wylde jerked his head in the most miniscule show of approval—or acceptance.

What was that all about? Were they going to leave instead?

But no, Elizabeth immediately indicated the six chairs furnishing the tight rectangle he leased for an absurd amount of money. "Let it not be said that we routed you from your own box. Stay and join us."

What?

Thea was hauling on his arm, trying her damnedest to back him out of there. Daniel didn't budge. Had he heard aright?

Wylde gestured to the empty seats. "Aye, you must remain and partake of the performance with us. We insist."

Deuced if this night didn't beat all.

Lighting farts and scandalizing the ton by socializing his sister with his tart.

Only Thea wasn't a tart.

She never had been. Not to him.

Which posed the question, what, exactly, was she?

WHILE THE DANCERS PRANCED ABOUT, everyone took their seats. Daniel positioned himself behind Ellie who sat next to Wylde. Thea he tucked securely on his opposite side, behind an empty chair.

Though he had the distinct impression not a one of them saw the ballet, all four heads remained fixed on the stage as though glued. Poor Thea, she'd approached the seat of her chair as if hot coals waited to fry her bum, her wide eyes imploring him not to participate in this farce.

But it wasn't a jest. Not to him. Or to his family.

Wylde and Ellie might be flirting with social disaster, but Daniel knew his sister didn't give a fig for expected behavior—their father had kept her on such a short chain during his lifetime, she was due whatever indulgence came her way. If associating for a single evening with a less-than-respectable female enlivened her life, then what was the harm? And Wylde? He already had a dubious reputation for flouting convention. As for himself, if a marquis couldn't savor the opera with the companion of his choice, then what was the use of a title?

Hoping he conveyed confidence, he reached over

to capture Thea's hand. Never taking his gaze from the exiting dancers, he untangled her fingers from the wreckage she'd made of her purse strings and wound his gloved fingers between hers. Giving a light tug, he repositioned their joined hands atop his thigh.

THE SECOND THE dancers disappeared off the stage, men and women exploded from their chairs and boxes to seek refreshment and recreation and, no doubt, urinary relief. The long interval between ballet and opera served several important purposes but its primary one, Daniel was certain, was to see and be seen. The surrounding melee was made more chaotic by the silence and the stillness that characterized the four of them.

No one moved, no one spoke.

Within seconds, the noise level beyond their silent foursome had increased tenfold.

Finally, some moments into the interval, Wylde nodded stiffly and excused himself.

The moment the door shut behind her husband, Ellie took the opportunity to fly into the empty seat next to Daniel.

"Is she the one?" his sister whispered behind her fan.

The one?

When Thea would have pulled away, Daniel tightened his grip on her hand. Keeping her firmly entrenched beside him, he cocked his head toward his sister, his blank look conveying, *The one what?*

Ellie leaned ever closer, flapped that fancy fan of hers ever faster. "The one who put the smile on your face," she said so softly he had to piece together the sentence. "The gouges...your neck."

A grin he couldn't stop gave her all the answer she needed.

She beamed back. Then her expression turned sardonic. Wafts from her fan brushed past his forehead as she inquired lightly, "Any chance she also revels in pounding your face? It looks rather atrocious, brother dear."

"Cream. More?"

"You need another jar of that latest batch? The one with the honeysuckle and cloves? Of course!" His sister's delight knew no bounds.

He wondered what she'd say if she knew he'd given all of his to Thea.

"I'll have it to you as soon as I gather some more and crush the blossoms. It's growing in the conservatory at the estate but it's too early for it to bloom outside— But you don't care about that." Her fan slowed to a crawl as she gave him a measuring glance. "I do believe this is the first time you've ever *asked* for more of a batch."

He shrugged, that was all.

"Bad night?" Ellie deduced. "Your voice?"

"The worst," he strained out.

"She's very elegant." Daniel nodded his agreement. "Refined too." Daniel nodded again. "Are you sure she's a lightskirt?"

He laughed outright. Then took a deep, cleansing breath and laughed again, just for the hell of it. Wonder of wonders, talking might seize him up like a fist clamped round his windpipe but laughter actually felt good.

His mirth drew Thea's gaze. Though her fingers trembled uncertainly within his, she gave him a sweet, almost demure smile, rendering him very, very glad they'd stayed.

To Thea's dismay, Lord Tremayne was called from their box a short time later, leaving her alone with the other woman, vastly curious what they'd just been whispering about.

Unsure where to look, after that too-brief, reassuring clasp of his hand to her shoulder, Thea flashed an uncertain glance past the empty chair between them. When she found the woman staring at her intently, Thea decided she found the stage below worthy of her complete fascination.

Pity nothing much was occurring on it.

Desperately, she looked into the orchestra pit. The musicians were pausing there as well, abandoning chairs and instruments in a bid to stretch their legs.

"Botheration! This will never do," the woman exclaimed, sliding over to sit directly beside Thea. "I know it's not done but I should like to meet you. I'm

Elizabeth, Daniel's sister." She gave a light laugh. "Lady Wylde, if I'm to do it right, but I've never been one to stand on ceremony, so please do call me Elizabeth. Neither have I ever seen him so happy. My brother, that is. Thank you for that."

His sister. So much more than simply friends, then.

Despite the invitation, Thea could not bring herself to regard Lord Tremayne's relative so informally, but her genuine warmth loosened Thea's tongue. "Happy? Pray, you must have your men confused."

"As though I have so many!" Lady Elizabeth smiled sincerely. "You're such a wit."

Not hardly. "As to that, why thank me? I've done nothing—"

"Oh, but you have. Tell me, what has he shared about himself?"

"Ah..." Very little, she was shamed to realize. Casting about for a response that might satisfy, Thea blurted, "That he disdains poetry and likes orreries."

Heave me to Hertfordshire, is that all I know?

Nay, for you know he's kind and thoughtful and generous. Thea's fingers twitched as though recalling the feel of the sumptuous winter gloves he'd given her. She also knew he was strong and protective and tender when he was with her, and when he touched her body, it sang more notes than any accomplished opera singer.

I know he makes me feel special.

"Fancy that." Her companion's voice trilled with

glee. "He told you of his contraptions. Then you aren't a cabbagehead like his last— Pardon me. I should not have said that." Lady Elizabeth's unfashionably tanned face pinkened. Her agitation gave rise to a furious fluttering of her fan. "I do spells, well *gentle blessings* I prefer to think of them, with herbs and such, did you know?" No answer was necessary because the fan kept twitching, the ebullient woman kept talking. "As to his preoccupation with orreries, has he mentioned that fellow who's come to town to give some lecture or other? Daniel so looked forward to attending that. I know he regrets having to miss it."

Feeling adrift at the rapid topic swings, Thea asked, "What fellow? If he's to make a presentation on orreries, there's a chance I know of him."

"Truly? How grand!" Lady Elizabeth went on to explain about a "monstrous" orrery in Lord Tremayne's study and how it wasn't working properly. Upon learning the acclaimed clockwork expert was come to London, Daniel had made plans to hear him speak. "Only now he's doing a favor for my husband and will miss the lecture. And he was so wishing to gain insight on correcting whatever's wrong with it. Over the years, he's collected a number of working models, but this particular one is special, for it belonged to our grandfather."

Amid her flurry of fan and facts, Thea had pieced together enough to realize it must be Mr. Horatio Taft from Manchester, visiting and lecturing. "I do know him, a Mr. Taft, for he consulted with my late husband on a project or two. If you do not think it's overstepping my place, I could attempt to locate him and see whether he will be in town a while and could perhaps meet with Lord Tremayne another time."

Lady Elizabeth's face took on a glow that turned her from pretty to stunning. "Overstepping, pah. The reality of meeting this fellow would give Daniel no end of delight." She leaned in close and the fan finally stilled. "Tell me, though, has he told you anything more? About himself?"

Suddenly Thea felt as though she were walking a tightrope, wavering upon a fine line between passing and failing. What? What else was he supposed to have told her? "Nothing specific comes to mind," she finally said.

Lady Elizabeth's disappointment was palatable and Thea tumbled right off that rope. Crashed into inexplicable sadness.

Compelled to defend him, she offered, "In truth, he doesn't talk that much. Not when we're together, anyway. We seem to, ah, be busy doing-other-things," she finished swiftly, feeling a hot flush flare over her forehead. "But we have been exchanging wonderfully charming letters."

That confession brightened Lady Elizabeth's countenance. "Letters?"

"Aye, sometimes several in a day." Thea couldn't stop the chuckle that emerged. "He's quite entertaining, has a flair for funning me. I've never laughed so much."

"Fun?" Lady Elizabeth mused on the word. "I don't think I've ever thought of my older brother as such, not since we were children. He's typically far too busy getting his face bashed in to indulge in something as banal as fun."

Thea winced at the disgruntled tone. "On that, I can commiserate. I did notice his propensity for walking into fists. What's a munsons muffler? Do you know?"

"I haven't an inkling. Why?"

"'Tis simply something that was said the first night we met." Thea waved it off. "I keep meaning to ask him and— What?" She lowered her voice guiltily. "Why are you looking at me so?"

"Because you—you..."

"I what?"

"You're nothing at all like I expected. You're so—" Lady Elizabeth pressed her lips together, as though contemplating whether or not to finish her thoughts. She did—astounding Thea with, "Ladylike! You're good for him. I've never seen him smile so much—"

"Smile? He's been dour since he arrived tonight."

"I'm not only talking about tonight," Lady Elizabeth answered evasively. "As to that, I'm sure he's just worried about tomorrow. He's giving a speech. That's the favor to Wylde and speechifying is one talent my brother would rather not indulge in."

"Really? I hadn't noticed," Thea said dryly, and the two shared a brief laugh.

Then this composed female of elevated station,

one who Thea never in a thousand years would have imagined actually conversing with, astonished her yet again. "I've had a brilliant idea—you can surprise him. If you're sincere about asking that orrery expert a favor, I'm sure nothing would mean more to my dear brother than to have the man drop by, assuming it works with his schedule, of course. Will you ask him?"

"Certainly. It would be an honor to please Lord Tremayne after all he's done for me," Thea assured, readily agreeing. "Only...well, to confess, I've no notion of his direction—if I'm able to contact him, where do I request Mr. Taft go?"

"That's easily remedied." Lady Elizabeth reached for her reticule with a bright smile. "I'll give you Daniel's address."

The players had taken the stage during the last few seconds. Music from the orchestra sounded and a full-voiced singer loosed the first notes while Thea watched her newest acquaintance retrieve pencil and paper.

Feeling the need to subdue the other woman's growing excitement, Thea cautioned, "Please realize that I've no notion of Mr. Taft's itinerary or whether his habits have changed. I do know where he stayed during prior visits, however, and I'll do my best to reach him tomorrow."

"That's perfect. All anyone can expect, really." Scribbling away, Elizabeth said, almost to herself, "Aye, I like this idea. You'll tell Daniel to stay at home and ask your Mr. Taft to call, while I—"

"*Tell* him to stay home? I think you overstate my influence on your brother."

"Do I?" She paused and turned to Thea, a look of consternation shading her features before they cleared and she flashed a conspiratorial smile. "I'm sure even mistresses become, ah...indisposed at times. If that's what he believes for a short duration and the end result is his happiness, where would be the harm?"

Where indeed?

The men chose that moment to return, their conversation continuing in hushed whispers before Lord Tremayne resumed his seat beside Thea (only after his sister relinquished it with a bright smile).

Lord Wylde, Thea couldn't help but notice, chose to remain standing. During the first lull of the powerful singing, he leaned down. "We'll be going now. Tremayne. Ahh, Mrs. Hurwell, was it?" He straightened and said in a more commanding tone, "Elizabeth?"

Lord Wylde held out his arm as Daniel croaked, "N-now?" evidently as surprised as she that the other couple would leave just as the performance got underway.

"Aye," Wylde said resolutely, encouraging his wife to her feet when she seemed to hesitate. "We only came for the ballet anyway."

BALLOCKS.

Daniel was hard-pressed not to laugh at Wylde's

pronouncement. They were here for the ballet? He knew that to be a clanker of the first-order.

They'd only come to indulge Ellie's desire for opera but if Wylde wanted to leave him and Thea alone, who was he to argue?

Actually, to his utter amazement, when the two of them had quit the box during the interval, the only thing his friend said in regard to Daniel's new mistress was that "she appears a fetching little thing" and he hoped they got on well together. That and a cryptic remark that meeting her might be beneficial for Elizabeth and their marriage—of all things.

Not a word on the inappropriateness of it all.

Daniel couldn't decide if he was thankful on Thea's behalf or offended on his sister's. Shouldn't Wylde take more umbrage over the perceived slight to Ellie's reputation?

Shouldn't you be more concerned over your committee commitments tomorrow?

Gads. He'd rather grow horns than think of all the last-minute counsel and wording suggestions Wylde had shoved down his silent throat out in the corridor.

Horns? Pah.

Much, much better to sit here with his sweet Thea, basking in her presence, than to worry about tomorrow.

After the door shut behind the other couple, Thea fiddled again with her purse, tucking something inside. After placing it on an empty chair, she glanced up at him and leaned a few inches closer. "Your sister. She's a lovely woman."

Daniel nodded.

"I... We... What you must think of me." She floundered about, but her gaze never left his.

He reached over and captured her hand, took his time tugging off her dress gloves. Speaking to her elegant fingers, he willed his neck to relax. "Think you're lovely...too."

"But we were *talking* while you were gone." She sounded as though the offense warranted beheading. "I know I shouldn't have behaved so familiarly but—"

A slight squeeze of her fingers and her ramblings stilled. He met her gaze again. "She's...persuasive."

"Aye," Thea breathed out on a sigh. "Very. It was awfully forward, I know, even being here with her. I hope you don't think ill of me."

As if he could. He brought her bare fingers to his lips. "Never."

She blasted him with a smile so bright he jerked back.

God, how he needed that smile.

And not just for tonight, he was starting to realize. Tomorrow. Next week, next year. When he was fifty. A hundred.

He might have a driving need to bed her—and oh how he did—but it was that smile he was plain coming to *need*.

.   .   .

FOR THE NEXT several thousand heartbeats or so, Daniel gave himself over to the unexpected escape. In their private nook, listening to the dramatic levels of feeling being expressed in song, he discovered both bliss and solace.

With his eyes closed, and his senses attuned to the woman at his side, it was an easy thing to forget the strain gripping his neck. An easy thing to relax and simply be.

Without any conscious effort, he allowed the music to wash over him. The sheer pleasure his auditory senses reveled in, thanks to the deeply sung notes—never mind that they were nonsense as he'd never learned Italian—reached through his lugs and somehow touched his soul.

Despite the clash of instruments and the tragic tale being told so woefully, the sounds loosened the tension, softened the muscles, until he was sitting there, staring at the blackness behind his eyelids, seeing brightness everywhere around him, his body suspended somewhere between alert and drowsy, one of the most peaceful, calming things he'd ever experienced.

The mournful, moving voice approached another, more intense, crescendo, bringing the reluctant awareness that the performance approached its end. That realization, in itself, brought sorrow, gathered grief like a shroud into his being. So much anguish, so much euphoria.

To think, he'd missed countless performances such as this, such depths and pinnacles of emotion, all because he avoided people. Avoided possible confrontations, probable conversations.

He'd been doing his spirit a disservice.

As the final notes wound to a stirring, heart-wrenching close, Daniel blinked open heavy lids. As though pulled by a relentless magnet to seek her out, he turned to study Thea. Rapt, she stared at the stage. A single tear left a glistening trail down her exposed cheek. As he watched, she covered her lips with her hand and compressed damp lashes.

Overcome.

Though he felt the same, he couldn't bear witnessing her reaction.

Startled to find he still held her hand, he released it in order to wrap his arm around her and bring her close to his side. She tilted her head until it rested against his shoulder. He felt the breath go out of her on a shudder.

Long minutes later, neither of them had moved a speck. The stage had emptied, the deafening applause finally drifting to nothing but indistin-guishable shouts and murmurs as hundreds if not thousands of people clambered for the exits.

Daniel angled his head until it rested against the top of Thea's. He inhaled deeply, drawing her essence deeper into the cracks of his soul. Cracks he hadn't realized existed until unlocked by the phenomenal talent they'd just witnessed.

He thought she'd eventually pull away. Gain her feet, be keen to go. He knew he'd been deplorable company all evening.

But instead of making any move to join the noisy exodus, she only snuggled deeper into his side.

When had her arm curved around his waist? Her other hand come up to rest beneath his neckcloth? How long had her thumb rubbed a tender caress through his linen shirt, over his heart?

"I don't mind if we wait here until the crowds dissipate." Her quiet voice reached his ears. The gentle caress didn't stop. "One time I overheard two ladies in the shop complaining that it took over an hour just to exit and that one of them was, horror of horrors..." Thea pitched her voice to a whispered nasally screech, "*Groped most objectionably in the bargain!*"

He laughed. A bone-deep, belly-shaking chuckle as he hauled Thea sideways onto his lap, cupped her cheeks in both hands, and wiped away the dried remnants of tears. Staring into her soft eyes, his laughter faded.

He should tell her, explain his mood.

The very atmosphere around them made him feel buoyant, as though the evening, and last few somber notes had lifted his spirit, lightened his load. Lessened the ever-present strain to the point where he felt like *talking*. Who knew when he might be so inclined again?

"There's a t-*task*—" Damn. *Take your time, Daniel.* His grandfather's voice, Everson's too. *There's no reason to rush.* "Task, an onerous one, I must see...to. Weighing on me and—"

And God, I need to see you smile.

Thea waited so patiently for him to mutter through. Stared at him so solemnly. Left off rubbing his chest to finger his newly shaved jaw with such a sense of discovery.

Had he really kept himself so closed off from her?

"In truth, I nn—" *Need* almost never tripped him up, never. Sod it—why now?

He had to tell her. All of it. "Explain!" burst out. "I like you, Thea, very much, and...because of that, nn—" *Need to tell you why I'm such an ogre sometimes.*

Goddammit. Why now?

As though she sought to interpret his butchered speech, her brow knit. "Are you pleased? Having me as your mistress?"

He gave a brief, wholly inadequate nod.

"Do you, ah, have any inclinations to end or alter our arrangement?"

Hell, no! An abrupt shake of his head had to suffice.

"You're completely justified, I know, if that is your wish."

He shook his head so hard his teeth rattled.

She still looked perplexed, so he tried again. "You d-d—" *Don't understand, damn me, I'm trying to tell you—*

"'Tis all right" She shushed him with a hug. Her words brushed his ears like velvet. "I know speaking of finer emotions is difficult if not impossible for the masculine sex. Say no more. Your actions speak more clearly than any I've known before. You care about my happiness and that means the world to me. I care about yours too."

After delivering that little, very welcome speech, she leaned back, eyes bright, her expression sweetly expectant. She was so understanding. So clueless. If she had an inkling—

Buxom Betsy bouncily brings brimming buckets of butter to bossy, blighted Bob. My ballocks are boiling for you.

"Been a bear tonight." Hallelujah! "Forgive me?"

"*Pffft.* There's nothing at all to forgive. You may not have been the soul of joviality but neither have you been mean or harsh." She patted his cheek. "Just frowny."

Which made him smile.

"Oh! You have a dimple. I don't believe I've seen it before."

"'Twas hiding."

"It surely was." She leaned forward to kiss the elusive dimple.

Daniel hadn't the fortitude to tell her what he'd meant: *he'd* been hiding.

Still was.

Still intended to if she kept looking at him as she did when she pulled back. "Tell you what," she posed, her eyes glittering emeralds as she stared at him. "For every frown I counted, I shall take a kiss. *Voilà.* They will be erased forevermore."

Then by God, let them get started. "How many?"

"I do believe I counted seventeen frowns, eight scowls and two snarls."

He couldn't help it. Damned if he didn't laugh again. Two *snarls*? *I've been a grump indeed.* "Seems I have much...to atone."

"Seems I am due many kisses. Now do you simply want to jaw about them all night or start delivering—"

The little minx thought to turn bossy on him? How adorable.

Daniel's mouth swooped to capture hers. He meant to tease, to tread lightly. He meant to nibble and savor. To suck gently upon her lips, entice her tongue out for a flirtation.

He did none of that. Pure want drove him now.

He thrust his tongue past her lips and hers slid forth to meet it. As they rubbed along each other, her fingers pushed through his hair, nails sank into his scalp.

His broad hand smoothed down her back to settle at her waist. His fingers clenched—just above the womanly flare of her arse.

Suddenly he was strangling to draw breath. A lingering swipe of his tongue along the roof of her mouth and he tore his head back. Gulped for air.

"One," she said on an equally loud breath. "Sixteen more to go—"

With powerful motions of his legs, he scooted his chair backward until it thumped against the closed door, hid them deep into shadows. No one would interrupt what he'd needed all night. *Her.* Completely.

"Want you." He sounded like a deuced caveman.

Her lips trembled but her eyes shone clear. "Then take me."

Before he could debate further with his conscience—frisking Thea in public had not been his plan when they'd set out earlier—she took the decision from him. She leaned forward to claim his lips, whispering just before they touched, "And now for two..."

The kiss was voracious, lacking restraint or finesse. Her tongue dueled with his as she murmured deep in her throat. As for Daniel, he couldn't get enough of her, couldn't slow the sensual onslaught. *Overpower and take. Take her and drown yourself,* seemed to be the litany commanding his actions.

He shifted Thea until she was astride him, wrenching that froth of sea blue higher until her thighs were bared atop the stockings. Her pale thighs, silken skin he couldn't wait to touch.

Only he couldn't stop framing her face with his hands, cupping her cheeks, threading his fingers through the elaborate sweep of hair. Couldn't bring himself to relinquish her precious face long enough to explore the tempting dainties below. Her nails scraped over his jaw as she tilted his head to the side, brushed lips and then teeth over his cheek and chin, down his neck.

"Love the scent you wear, always have," she told him just before applying suction to a part of his neck that inflamed his entire body. He stiffened *everywhere.*

Scent bedamned, he had to be in her, seize her against him or go mad trying. Were those her impatient fingers grappling with the fall of his breeches, slipping inside to stroke his length? Her fingers tightening into a fist around his shaft as he gave a ragged groan?

Had to be, he thought distractedly as he became aware of pure decadence, silky hot and sinfully sweet when his intrepid fingers journeyed far, fatalistically far from her head and—to his dismay and delight—met beneath the plump halves of her arse. Met and slid boldly along the seam between.

Where were her drawers? He was touching skin. Hot, humid skin he was so damn hungry for—

Breath labored, Thea's clasp on his cock jerked. Her whimper came soft but unmistakable.

Don't do it, some prudent part of his brain cautioned.

Oh, aye, do it, the flex of her bum encouraged.

Coated with her heat, his hands kneaded the firm flesh of her flanks, delved a bit farther into the crevice.

"May I..." His voice was a croak. He firmed his resolve and his palms, stretched his fingers just a wee bit more and was rewarded when her constricting anus met the tip of his longest finger. Daniel circled the digit around the puckered ring. *Play here...* "Linger?"

"Ahh. Um... Should I let you?" she breathed hotly against his neck. "Would a..." *Mistress allow it?*

He could just hear her mind asking the questions—*Do mistresses truly do this? Or is it too tawdry? Totally taboo?*

Will I be no better than a hedge whore or street doxy—

But then her hold tightened on his shaft and her luscious derrière rotated beneath his finger, answering for her, even before she said in a low whisper, "All right."

He exhaled in relief and spread his grip over her arse cheeks, loving the feel of the warm flesh against his palms. His middle finger? It wasn't going anywhere. Except deeper. When he navigated the perimeter of the impossibly tight ring, exploring both her body and the boundaries of what she might accept, she pulled his penis taut.

Pressure seized his groin. Longing filled his loins.

Longing to tell her what she meant to him, what exploring her like this did to his body, his mind, his heart—

"Is it terribly wicked? For us to do *this* here? Now?" Upon uttering *this*, she angled her body and his, rocking her hips until his stiff and ready prick was nudging along slick folds.

To strum her, *here* of all places. A private box he'd purchased to salve his conscience and his past. A past that receded far into the shadows when she squirmed her creamy center against him again.

Daniel swore. Good God Almighty—he was close to exploding and wasn't even in her yet. Not properly.

The hot cave of her arse threatened to suck him into its depths. He was sweating, drenched in desire.

Do it, he wanted to tell her, *take me inside. No one will interrupt.*

His damn finger—hell, his whole arm—shook with the force he exerted not to plunge it into forbidden territory.

Thea shifted forward, sliding along his shaft until reaching the crown. A slight wiggle of her pelvis and his cock eased into her as though greased.

She gasped, her feminine muscles pulling him deeper yet clinging together so tightly it was a marvel he could gain any friction at all. When she said, "Terribly wicked for you to touch me *there*," and surged up, then back down, her feet on the floor giving her leverage, damned if her nock didn't open and invite his finger in as well.

"T-terribly." He covered the blunder by latching on to the smooth skin just beneath her ear. Deliberately teasing, he stifled the urge to move—he was liable to nail her to the ceiling if he let his body have its way. Speaking against her skin, he mused, "Shall I stop? With...draw and re...turn you home?"

Any answer she might have made changed to a gasp when he sucked harder. But as he eased the suction and plied his tongue over the succulent spot, she painted rainbows in his sky with her response. "Nay. 'Twould be a crime, for I believe I like being wicked with you here and now. Maybe later too.

"And not to belabor the point..." Every orifice he'd entered rippled against him as she spoke, enticed him to move, so he resisted. "But those snarls still need erased, I'll have you know."

When he made a sound in his throat, she consoled. "Not that I'm complaining, my lord…"

He swore her pelvis jerked against him in all the right places. Pulling him inward from both directions. "Not at all," she offered on another gasp, her lips pressed to the newly sensitive skin of his jaw. "In fact, I understand about tonight. Your sister explained your mood."

It wasn't quite being dunked in an icy lake, but it was close. He tried to articulate but only managed a grunt. "Eh?"

"She said you perform a favor for Lord Wylde tomorrow, a troublesome one." Those lithesome legs of hers lifted her up, then sank her loins back to his, gave a tiny hitch that buried him up to his ballocks. The wave of lust that rolled over him at the sinuous motions threatened to swamp him. "So I understand your fit of the sullens. 'Twill be over in mere hours, though, aye?"

Fit of the sullens? And now he sounded like a grouchy lad of eight. "Sulks b-b—" *Be gone,* dammit!

But her lips vanquished the urge to speak. And the lands south of her hips promised heaven if he would but listen. "'Tis more kisses you owe me, my lord. There's the matter of several scowls… Besides, wicked or ruinous, or tawdry beyond reckoning"—she tightened around him and her breath caught when she lifted to slide along his cock again—"I don't care if it is, not tonight."

Daniel thought he heard a shred of guilt—tempered with defiance, perhaps—but he couldn't have held back, not any longer. Not when he was drowning in such taboo sexual bliss with such an outwardly decorous and demure young woman.

Not when—

Her lower body soared and jerked against his groin, directing, if not controlling, his thrusts. Positioned over him as she was, Thea, his sweet, sexually shy Thea took command.

"Harder," she whispered, swinging her pelvis against him in a tempest of need.

One his body echoed. So he canted his groin until her every downward plunge took him to the root.

She started to squeal, then muffled her lips against his cheek. "Don't stop. Don't ever stop," or something similarly needy emerged.

His fingers took the message to heart. The buried one pulled free and snared a mate. Then the two of them poised to enter, circling the entrance to the hot cavern made slippery by her trickling juices. The ring of her anus was open now, the muscles slightly lax. With just a slight push, both fingers slid past that first constriction; with a firmer nudge, and the friction that his back-and-forth motion created, they sank deep.

And his prim mistress turned into a cavewoman —tugging on his hair, pummeling the muscles of her moist, private places against their invaders, clutching and clasping at him as he pumped fingers and cock both. Sweat rolled from his temples onto her desperate countenance as she marauded and plundered his neckcloth until she could kiss and suck—and bite—the skin lining his neck and collar.

"Ah-oh— Ahh!"

In tandem with her breathy cries and tensing muscles, he ground his fingers into her arse, bucked his ballocks against her buttocks and lunged faster and fiercer, more connected with her, on so many levels, than he ever had been with another. Ever could be.

Oh God. Oh gads.

What was wrong with him?

Why ponder *emotional* closeness when his prick was busy prigging? Time to apply himself to taking his pleasure, by damn.

Only, for once, it didn't seem to matter. Because though he'd long forgotten how to breathe, had been seeing stars and spots and dancing little hearts for some time now, and though his wrist ached and fingers had gone numb, he didn't slow or pause or think to stop. Not until Thea screamed—*screamed*, by damn—and melted over his groin. Not until her arse sucked him so far inside, she promised a home to any and every part of him that ever existed.

Not until he'd pleasured her so thoroughly that she went limp did he give serious thought to taking his own satisfaction.

Only he'd already found it.

Oh, not because he'd peaked—he hadn't, not yet (though bridling the urge nearly did him in)—but because he'd found *his* satisfaction by *giving* Thea hers.

Was that a noose he felt tightening around his neck?

Was that why his brain box had succumbed to fevered chills?

Was this love, the deep, abiding kind he'd never sought, never expected? The overpowering, over-whelming emotion that made fools of men? That made his gut churn with nausea, his beleaguered brain with bopping, bobbing B's? Bouncing Betties and beaming Bobs?

His mind overfloweth with nonsense, his heart with peace. Could love truly be that capricious? That fantastically fickle?

Nay, he assured himself, trying to remember how to draw breath. *Nay!*

'Twas simply tupping the delectable Thea that addled his wits. That was all. A good swiving with a fine mistress likely boggled finer men than him.

After his body crested the pinnacle, an explosive event that took mere seconds to reach once he quit battling the urge, instead of offering recriminations or calling him base and screeching obscenities at him for his obscene behavior, his prim and lusty little mistress only blinked at him wearing a dazed smile.

"Well now." She blinked again, smiled a bit brighter. "I must say, *I* certainly did not mind being groped in that wholly *un*-objectionable manner."

Then, lips and body trembling, she shakily eased

off him and to her feet and started riffling inside her bodice. "Here." She produced a wad of padding that left her bosom decidedly uneven. "Have some cotton. I'm afraid I left you all sticky."

While he sat, benumbed and blighted (were Cupid's arrows poison tipped? he wondered), she proceeded to use the stuffing from the other side's enhancement to clean herself.

And a noose had never felt more welcome.

2

A BIT OF PATHETIC POETRY

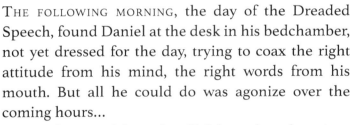

THE FOLLOWING MORNING, the day of the Dreaded Speech, found Daniel at the desk in his bedchamber, not yet dressed for the day, trying to coax the right attitude from his mind, the right words from his mouth. But all he could do was agonize over the coming hours...

Not because his neck still felt as though a viper had sunk in its fangs—a single night's sleep had restored his muscles to their customary, on-the-edge-of-tense state; thankfully, they felt no worse for all of yesterday's use—but because he knew he should care more about Wylde's cause.

And frankly, he didn't. Despite his efforts, he couldn't seem to foment any excitement.

His thoughts—his easily aroused excitement—remained squarely with his mistress. She'd sent round a note early this morning by way of Swift

John. For once, instead of lingering for a reply, the servant had delivered the letter along with a message that reached Daniel via his butler: "I've a number of errands to run for Miss Thea and will return for any response by nuncheon. Better yet, send John later; his lazy legs could use the jaunt."

Though the sibling jibe had lightened his mood, it hadn't helped his concentration. The neatly folded and wax-sealed square beckoned hordes more than his speech notes.

Notes he'd studiously avoided all morning.

He tapped the edge of Thea's letter against his desktop, sorely tempted to tear into it. "Nay. Use it for incentive."

That was it! He'd review his planned phrasing three times more, the last out loud, before reading her note.

How he wished the day's events were done and over. But it was hours still until the damn meeting. Until his part in it was complete and he could visit her again.

"Enthusiasm," he muttered, reluctantly relinquishing her missive, "need t-to garner some."

"Woof!"

He patted Cy's head, scratched the dog's chin. Wiped the drool on his handkerchief and decided to go about it another way. He located the sheet Everson had written. He'd practice two letters aloud (no sense in overdoing), *then* apply himself to the business of reviewing his speech.

Paul was a pea-goose, a pink of the ton, yet his profound penis promised pleasure to every pudding-headed puss and Pocket Venus on the planet.

Willie had a wee little weedle, but when he grew into Walt, the girls were in alt, for what once was wee could now wiggle and wow!

After reciting the pair of ribald selections, instead of studying the compelling reasons Wylde had so passionately set forth, Daniel couldn't stop his pen from doing a little composing of its own:

There once was a pebble in my shoe.
Cows go moooooooooooooooo.

I once knew a cat,
with a sniveling nose,

"What now?" Testing options, he scratched out *hedgerows, pose, close, grows* and *sews*, frowned, and then chose to move on to more colorful pastures.

Roses are red,
Mr. Freshley was a snoacher
then a poacher and

"Deplorable, D-Daniel! Wretched, sodding po-poetry."
But then inspiration struck.

Roses are red,
Your name is Dorothea.
It pains me to say it,
so I changed it to Thea.

"Nay. Too pat." Thinking aloud, he rewrote the last line. "...Name is D-Dorothea. It p-pains me to say it, so I chopped it in half."

There. That brought a smile, and at the man's third knock, Daniel finally allowed his valet to enter and begin the task of outfitting him properly. This included a fresh scrape of any whiskers that dared emerge since yesterday's "sculpting" (why Crowley didn't just call it shaving, Daniel didn't know), complaints about the missing jar of Lady Wylde's latest concoction—known officially as The Miraculous Bruise Vanishing Cream (this nomenclature too from his valet)—and a neckcloth arrangement so intricate, it could hold its own in a contest against Brummell's.

A quick glance in the mirror and Daniel was set.

Still rather pleased with himself for his poetic (if pathetic) turn of phrase where Thea was concerned, feeling lighter than he had all morning, he dismissed Crowley and whisked through his speech notes with nary a slip (shouldn't be too surprising as he'd eliminated most anything likely to incite a stammer).

Relieved at the sense of accomplishment, he reached for Thea's letter.

My dear Lord Tremayne,

He really needed to tell her to call him Daniel.

*There stands so much I'd like to say but as I know you
have commitments today, I shall endeavor to brevity (do
stop laughing at me, if you please; I mean it this time—
for yours is valuable).*

*Let me just convey my sincere appreciation for what
proved to be a most exceptional evening. (Though I do
tend to find myself thinking the same following every
incidence of spending time together.)*

*I confess, when Sarah first suggested our illicit arrange-
ment, I could never have anticipated that I would find
such a valued and cherished companion in the bargain.*

*I knew I'd been lonely and that things were becoming
more dire than I wanted to admit (even to myself). But
you, why... Well, having you in my life has made what I
thought was my last, most reluctantly agreed to (and
dare I admit it, desperate) option into one of the most
freeing and splendorous experiences of my life. (I blush,
but 'tis true, and so I have admitted it. Dear me, where is
a fresh breeze when a girl needs to cool her cheeks?)*

Your well-pleasured mistress, Thea

*PS. Despite your apparent dread last evening pertaining
to today's events—*

That gave him pause. *Dread.* Had his disinclination been so very obvious? For one used to masking their inner selves, 'twas a sobering revelation.

Or was it just Thea who could read him so?

Eager to escape his thoughts, he turned to the remaining lines.

...apparent dread...today's events, I have every confidence in you. I know you'll succeed in your efforts and look forward to your realization of the same.

PS. Once Again—I have a full day planned as well and a most peculiar appeal: If you'll indulge me, and forgive me for being so impertinent, please stay at your residence tonight. Possibly tomorrow night as well. Something your sister mentioned inclines me to think she's engaged in arranging a surprise for you, one that can only come to successful fruition if you remain home-bound in the evening.

Though "peculiar" didn't begin to describe her last request, it was the paragraph before that commanded his attention: *I have every confidence in you. I know you'll succeed...*

Her blind faith in him pulled the scales from his eyes. Light so painfully bright shone into his being and illuminated the truth bursting from his heart. He loved her.

He utterly and totally loved her, by damn.

Doubt, nausea and nooses aside, by all that was

holy and hellacious, he'd fallen in love with his mistress.

LONG BEFORE THE sun rose that morning, Thea had toiled over two of the three notes she'd sent out by way of Buttons. Composing the one to Mr. Taft had been as simple as drawing a dot. Either he'd be reachable or not. Either he'd remember her or not. Either he'd be inclined to grant her request or...

Or she'd be vastly disappointed.

And Lord Tremayne would forever wonder why she was so presumptive as to disavow his presence two nights in a row by having the effrontery to order him to stay home.

As to that, the note to Lord Tremayne proved significantly more difficult to write than the brief missive to the respected clockmaker. When one has thousands of thoughts vying to be heard, how to select only a few to share? She managed well enough, or so she'd assured herself before superstitiously kissing the page (a good-luck gesture intended for the man who'd open it) and folding it shut with crisp, precise edges.

It was the third and last letter that her pen dithered over the most. The letter she'd composed in more than a cursory state of shock because when she'd arrived home hours before and crawled into bed, intending to commit Lord Tremayne's address to memory, what should her eyes be greeted with upon pulling from her reticule the card Lady Elizabeth had surreptitiously given her just before departing the box?

Not a simple address—which it did have.

But the hastily scrawled-upon card also contained an additional note, one that rendered Thea wide awake into the night: *Lord W is away most days from 10 until 6, often later. Please call upon me at your earliest convenience. 'Tis urgent.*

Urgent? Something Thea might assist with?

After scant hours of fitful sleep haunted by rampant curiosity, not to mention persistent recollections of the lusty encounter she'd just indulged in, Thea awoke without an answer. How exactly did one respond to such a note?

She debated and deliberated, paused and pondered.

In the end, she sent Buttons to deliver the other two, asking that he come back straightaway, determined to have decided before his swift feet brought him home.

Simply put, invited or not, Thea couldn't bring herself to show up at the woman's house, and she was reluctant to ask Sarah's advice. Thea was positive one *never* contacted the well-born sister of one's titled protector, but assumed, as with tinkering with Mr. Hurwell's cuckoo clocks, 'twould be easier to ask for penance than permission.

And perhaps, Lady Elizabeth enjoyed writing as much as her brother?

Lady Wylde—

Was that the proper address? Once upon a time, Thea's mother had begun teaching Thea all she'd learned from finishing school, manners and etiquette and how to address those with titles, but the lessons had ceased when Mama became ill and crossed over to another existence.

Much worse than an incorrect salutation, what if the note was delivered to Lady Elizabeth's husband first? Mr. Hurwell always insisted upon reading and approving any correspondence Thea sent or received, likely why she'd lost touch with her few remaining friends shortly after her marriage. She'd wondered more than once whether her letters even made it across the threshold.

Best assume prying eyes might, well...*pry*.

All right then...

Lady W—

If it is not overly presumptive, I would request that you visit me at your convenience. Since you indicated this was a matter of some urgency, I will endeavor to remain home for the next three days

Or should that be two days? That trip to Seven Dials Thea kept putting off weighed on her; her rent might be paid through the following weekend, but who knew whether Grimmett would honor it?

the next ~~three~~ two days (in their entirety) and you may
call at your leisure. My household tends to rise early, so
do not fear

"Thea," she gritted out between clenched teeth, shaking her quill over the wordy missive and speckling it with ink, "keep it *brief*."

Ever mindful of the expense, for paper was precious regardless that it was no longer her purse making the purchase, she folded, creased, and then carefully ripped the page free of her ink-blotched blathering.

Lady W—

Please call upon me at your convenience. Any day or time
this week is agreeable.

T.H.

"MA'AM?"

As well he might, Buttons looked startled by her request upon his return.

Thea strove to appear calm and in full possession of her faculties. "Aye. This one is intended for Lady Wylde, Lord Tremayne's sister." Buttons just kept staring and Thea's lips kept flapping. "If it helps, I met her last night and she asked *me* to *call* on her. I'm sending this instead." Thea thrust the labored-over note into his safekeeping.

Diffident now, he nodded. "O' course. Know jus' where she's at, not that you need bother explaining your actions to *me*. I'm just your humble servant."

"Of course not," Thea said dryly. "You tell me that *after* I've babbled a defensive explanation."

With a wink, he was off, leaving Thea to debate anew whether she'd made the right decision.

Ah, well.

Time would tell.

Time that moved wretchedly slowly as every second seemed to expand the longer she waited for a reply. Surprisingly, it was that dot-easy missive that caused her the most unease. Would Mr. Taft remember her? Would he be willing to accommodate the unusual request?

And how many more times could she circle her small entry before wearing through the floor and finding herself instantly dropped into the kitchen? Fortunately it was not a question she'd answer today, for at just that moment, not only did her brazen cuckoo clock gong, bong, chime and chirp, but the knocker on the front door sounded. One of her notes bearing fruit, perhaps?

AFTER RECEIVING Lady Elizabeth in her sedate morning room (hoping the woman had turned a blind eye to the decor on the way), pouring tea and exchanging pleasantries, Thea thought she'd be treated to the reason for this most unusual visit.

Only Lady Elizabeth seemed more inclined to relive last night's adventure, speaking vibrantly of the ballet dancers, the opera (which was odd, given how her husband ushered her out shortly after it started), the crowds, her most "prodigiously happy brother", orreries, speeches, more on the ballet dancers…

Even when moneyed females had deigned to step into Mr. Hurwell's shop, Thea had never seen more elegant daytime attire. Clothed in a pale blue walking dress with a double layer of some fancy lacework at the bottom, Lady Elizabeth managed to look both cool and composed.

Though her visitor chattered away and appeared concerned with nothing more than light gossip and fashion (she'd just begun describing the magnificent opera dress worn by some woman Thea had never heard of), Thea couldn't help but notice the dirt smudged into her slippers and the grass stain on the edge of her double-flounced hem—and the sprig of lavender defying Lady Elizabeth's repeated efforts to tuck it neatly away in her reticule.

What secrets lurked behind the dirt-dusted slippers and speedy sentences sallying forth?

When her guest's third monologue (this one enumerating all of her brother's admirable qualities) showed no signs of abating, Thea decided to implement her newfound habit of speaking what was on *her* mind. "Pardon my boldness, but we both know you didn't come over here so expediently to talk solely of last night or your brother."

Granted the woman had been all that was amiable and affable, issuing none of the warnings or dire predictions Thea had secretly feared. *'Tis a passing fancy,* she'd dreaded hearing. *Certainly, he likes you now, but expect naught next week. Naught but him tiring of you.*

Broooohahaha-ha-ha-ha!

Demonic monsters and armor-attired mice had run amok through her dreams. Shaking off the residual trepidation, Thea implored, "Tell me, what is so vital you risk visiting a woman of disrepute?"

"Please, do not put yourself down so. You are the *perfect* person to help me with my little predicament. Well, I confess, 'tis not so little. It's grown to epic proportions over the last few days, becoming a most Dire Dilemma."

"Whatever it is I shall provide whatever assistance I can."

"Oh," Lady Elizabeth exhaled on a gust. "I knew I could depend upon you! 'Tis a simple matter really..."

"Aye?" Thea prompted when no more was forthcoming.

"Teach me how to be a mistress."

As though a flood of mud clogged her hearing, thickened her tongue and sludged her breathing, Thea slowly enunciated, "You...would...like...*me*...to...do...what?"

Lady Wylde didn't fidget, didn't demure. Her feet

remained firmly on the floor, hands folded in her lap. She presented a serene, dignified manner that on the surface appeared everything that was proper. And when she spoke, her words were clear as glass. "Mrs. Hurwell. Thea." But her cheeks bloomed like a rose. "I need you to tell me, precisely, how to go about being a mistress. A spectacular one."

Once Thea quit laughing (which took rather awhile) she attempted, as delicately and decisively as possible, to explain this wasn't exactly a position she'd held long, nor one in which she claimed prodigious experience. "Truly, I am muddling through one encounter at a time."

"But you must be doing it right! I've never seen Daniel so relaxed, so buoyant."

"I'm tickled to hear it, but—"

"There must be *someone* we can ask," Lady Elizabeth said earnestly as though discussing how to cultivate loose sexual behavior was as humdrum as hemlines. "Someone you know who can give me lessons. Pointers. Guidelines." Now she was beginning to lose her polish, as her words came faster and more frantic. "Or just a vague indication of how to behave in a sultry and alluring manner. I'm not overly particular but I need assistance, I tell you! Instruction so I can seduce my husband before he wanders!"

And then the whole story spilled out—how Lady Elizabeth's husband expected *her* to be his mistress (else he'd find another, or so Thea gathered, secretly thinking the man's methods seemed rather sweet but keeping her opinion to herself as Lady Elizabeth's agitation grew).

Eventually Thea rose and placed a calming hand on the other woman's shoulder. "Never fear, we'll find someone," she assured with pure bravado because she'd just recalled Sarah was away from London, visiting family. *Think, Thea!*

She straightened and began to pace. Who—

When the lavender spike peeking out from Lady Elizabeth's reticule again caught her attention, she no longer had to feign confidence, a pair of stockings that exact color flashing through her mind. "I have it. I know just the person! She's young but enthusiastic."

At the pronouncement, Lady Elizabeth's face noticeably brightened, then turned a bit puzzled. "Enthusiastic? About..."

"Sex," Thea said plainly, hoping Buttons knew how to direct her new coachman to wherever Anna and, by association she'd learned the night of Sarah's party, Susan resided.

⚊⚊⚊◗◖⚊⚊⚊

"THAT WAS POORLY DONE, Dan. Poorly done indeed. The way you treated Everson's boy Tom was abominable! *You let me down.*"

Those were Penry's greeting words, delivered like a death knell, when he walked into Daniel's study after Rumsley showed him in.

After his cryptic note and absence, Daniel had

expected to hear from him eventually—either an explanation or the requesting of one. But he'd assumed it would come by letter-bearing footman.

Penry had an aversion to dog drool, something he'd admitted after Cy sniveled over and ruined his second pair of buckskins. And since Daniel had an aversion to visiting any abode with six chirping women in residence, the man's friendship was maintained primarily through correspondence, bouts at Jackson's, and the rare meet at their club.

"Braving Cyclops," Daniel mused, as Penry barreled toward him where he sat at his desk. When his visitor reached it, instead of taking a chair, Penry remained standing, breathing fire. Daniel tilted his head to make eye contact. "Damn. Must be important in-d-d-*deed*."

"Right, it's important, you insolent pup," Penry roared. "I would have been here sooner, much sooner, else for those blasted offers. And tears—buckets of them! They cry if they don't call, they cry if too many do and now— But no, let me not quibble about like a nagging woman.

"I can't stay long," Penry grated out, indignation expanding his chest. "Have an appointment with one of the bucks angling after Eliza. Then there's the committee vote this afternoon."

Penry paused and glanced down, took another, evaluating, look at Daniel's face. "That was accommodating of you—I see you let someone do my job for me and throttle you senseless."

"Let?"

"Come now, we both know no one gets in that many jabs against you unless you allow it. Nevertheless, Dan"—his eyes narrowed to slits and it wouldn't have surprised Daniel to see smoke coming from his ears—"that haughty air you cultivate to avoid others sometimes works to your detriment, if you would but see it! Everson thinks you do not like him."

Startled by that, Daniel protested. "I like him fine. B-better than most." Especially now.

"When are these blamed things going to wind down?" Penry gestured toward the rotating mechanisms abounding at the moment. Trying to come to grips with his recent revelation regarding his mistress—and his *feelings* toward said mistress, Daniel had paced his study, winding up and starting every orrery he owned; the functioning models that was, his prime machine still limped along sadly in the center of the room.

After getting them all going, he'd lounged in his chair to enjoy the show.

"Maggots, one and all!" Penry frowned at a sprightly, spinning tabletop unit as though it were responsible for every unwanted gentleman caller he'd suffered that week. "Distracting as hell!"

Daniel remained silent. Let Penry get it all out; he'd obviously stewed himself into a frenzy.

"Fine! Don't answer me but I'll not leave without telling you this—that boy you disillusioned—he near idolizes you. Has since the Dover match back in oh eight. He was eleven, Dan, *eleven* when he saw you then. Think, man! As far back as that, Tom wanted to make your acquaintance and his father put him off. I told Everson to bring him around Jackson's more than once but you know what he said?"

Daniel opened his mouth to explain how he'd already taken care of things but Penry was on a roll that showed no signs of slowing. "Dammit! He said he respected you too much to spring Thomas on you and didn't want to offend you by asking. Offend you, by God, by *asking* you to meet his boy!" Penry shoved Cyclops away when a clear line dribbled from the side of his smiling mouth, causing a dark spot to appear near Penry's knee.

"I was wrong."

Penry hadn't heard him, was too caught up in his own ire. "Damn you, Dan. I know how they wronged you—I saw it, lived through watching it, which was deuced bad enough. I cannot imagine how it tore you to pieces. But they're gone now, Robert and your father. They're gone. And you're turning into them!"

His blow delivered, Penry glared at him in the echo of the ticking orreries. Had Daniel been kindling, he knew he would've ignited.

Cy barked, filling in the silence.

"Now compose your thoughts." Penry took a few agitated steps. "You're not getting rid of me until I hear something sensible from you—and I'm not talking about *how* you talk, but what you say."

"I know." His murmur went unheard because Penry called for Cyclops and tossed a rag to the other side of the room.

Things must be dire indeed if Penry would stoop

to playing with his dog. Daniel pushed back from his desk and went to them.

"I know," he said again, louder. "Agree with everything you say. T-Tom—he's worse off than I ever was, but in ways that count, he's b-better. B-because of his family. Because of Everson. I'm jealous."

"Then go tell him that." Penry threw the toy again. Cy bounded after it (as much as his lazy hide could bound), thrilled with his new playmate. "If anyone would understand your need for privacy, it's them."

He started to tell his friend it was all taken care of, but as it was the first time Penry had ever laid into him—outside the ring—Daniel chose to keep silent. Let Penry think he'd changed Daniel's mind, convinced him how to proceed.

Lord knew it was flattering to be taken to task by someone who cared. Someone who did it without cruelly cutting words or slashing canes. "I will. Soon."

Yesterday, in fact, Daniel thought with a secret smile.

Satisfied, Penry nodded. Then he grinned like the devil. "And now to tell you why else I came round—I've arranged a little celebration tonight. It's in your honor though no one else knows."

"Celebration?" For today's upcoming speech? "I haven't d-done anything yet. Who knows if it will b-be successful?"

"As to that, who cares? This is Wylde's cause. I'm

just in on it to annoy the hell out of Bolden." Cy barked happily when Penry circled the rag over his head before flinging it to the side. "I swear he cheated that time he won my greys off me. For tonight, I'm celebrating you—this is the first time you've ventured putting yourself on any public stage, no matter how small, and I'm proud of you. It's about damn time you quit hiding behind your desk or these planets." Penry flicked a tiny turquoise Earth that had clicked to a standstill.

When Cy dropped the rag at his feet, Penry bent to toss it again. Straightening, he glanced at his pocket watch. "I really need to— Hell, Eliza's buck can stew," he said, coming over to take one of the seats flanking the desk.

Eyes lit with an unholy light, Penry imparted, "I saw fit to organize another shadow play. Know how much you like them. Donaldson found a new female —some chit over from Germany, I think. Must be, goes by the name *Fräulein* Wunderbar Ober- schenkel, if you can believe it."

Rather than correct his friend (it was Louise who'd favored that particular style of entertainment, not Daniel) and relieved the harangue was over, he walked back to his desk, settling in the companion chair. In *front* of the desk, not behind it, though he suspected Penry might still be too worked up to notice—only for altogether different reasons now.

Penry was grinning, almost daring Daniel to try and pronounce that mouthful. Wunderbar Ober- schenkel? He knew better. "Which means...?"

"Best I can gather, it's something like Miss Splendid Thighs."

That brought a much-needed laugh. "What? Does she p-perform tricks with them? Like...pick up...grapes?"

"Now wouldn't that be something! I haven't heard any particulars, other than the name is well earned, but I can't wait to find out. Can you imagine what type of show she must put on?"

Envisioning the possibilities, Daniel's loins started to grow heavy—but only for half a heartbeat. How could he expose Thea to something so tawdry? In truth, his own interest wasn't nearly as keen as it would have been a fortnight ago.

He might want to do tawdry things with his pretty mistress, but that didn't mean he wanted others knowing about them. Didn't mean he wanted to debauch her in public.

It was one thing if *he* showed her carnal pleasures beyond the norm; quite another if she learnt them elsewhere. But how to bow out gracefully?

As if he didn't already have enough weighing on him, the memorized lines in front of him, the *lack* of Thea tonight, the—

That was it!

Daniel shook his head with feigned regret. "Cannot. Thea's not available tonight."

"Not available?" Penry looked incredulous. "Don't let that stop you! She's your mistress, man, put her in her place. As to that, Sarah's off visiting her sister and you can be assured I'll still be there."

"To watch?"

When Cy nudged his knee, Penry pushed him away. "Or participate if *Fräulein* Wunderbar looks as wonderful as her namesake."

Participate? Daniel frowned. "What of Sarah?"

A snort came from Penry's direction. "What of her? She's comely and accommodating and I've rewarded her well for it. But it's not as if she's my wife. Furnishing that new house of hers set me back a coin or two, I tell you, so she's got nothing to complain about."

Cy whined at the loss of his playmate. Daniel snapped his fingers, calling the dog to him.

"I've been with her going on four years now. The old prick's getting peevish..." Penry rubbed his hands together like a lecher. Not an image that sat well with Daniel. "I've got to get my turn on the comely *fräulein*. Just the thought of taking a ride on those splendid thighs..."

Penry kept talking, and with every word, Daniel's inner disquiet grew. *It's not as if she's my wife.*

Penry's wife. A woman he left at home so he could ramble about with Sarah...

Sarah, who'd introduced Daniel to Thea.

Daniel sank his fingers in Cy's slathered-upon jowls, scratched for all he was worth. Loyalty. Shouldn't it be rewarded?

Loyalty. Faithfulness.

Never would he consider attending such a debauched event on his own—without Thea. To watch, much less participate.

So he declined. Suffered through Penry's vocal objections and declined again.

Bother it. Penry refused to listen, had some chaw bacon idea that Daniel had to attend or 'twould all be for naught.

"Will. *Halt*," Daniel thundered, finally gaining the other man's silence with his rarely used given name. "G-go. Enjoy. B-but 'twill be without me."

"Fine," Penry huffed, heading toward the door with a disparaging shake of his head. "'Tis your loss."

Damn. This visit might have begun with Penry announcing his displeasure with Daniel, but it was ending the opposite—with Daniel regarding his longtime friend with new eyes.

Had Penry always been this callous toward the women in his life?

Or was Daniel's relationship with Thea causing him to see things differently?

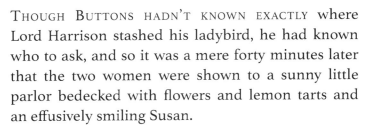

THOUGH BUTTONS HADN'T KNOWN EXACTLY where Lord Harrison stashed his ladybird, he had known who to ask, and so it was a mere forty minutes later that the two women were shown to a sunny little parlor bedecked with flowers and lemon tarts and an effusively smiling Susan.

Anna was out with Lord Harrison, leaving Susan in place as "Mistress of the Manor" she told them with a laugh as they gingerly took seats on the brocade couch she indicated and just as gingerly divulged the purpose of their visit.

"Really now? You two ladies want me to teach you how to be a mistress?" Thea noticed her H's were flowing much more smoothly. "If that don't beat a rug! I was just thinking the other day about writing a pamphlet on that very topic."

As she spoke, Susan very carefully poured tea for all three of them (Thea was still marveling at being called a *lady* and being lumped in the same category with Lady Elizabeth, however erroneous).

"'Course, it would help a heap if I knew my letters and could write." Susan laughed a tad self-consciously. She settled herself upon the remaining chair, with tea in hand and little finger daintily extended.

"I'll teach you," Lady Elizabeth promised quickly. "Or pen the pamphlet for you under your direction if you prefer, only please, tell me every-thing you can about how to be a mistress, a good one. And quickly. I don't know how much longer his patience will hold out."

"'E's not treating you rough, is 'e?" Susan dropped her effort at gentility and did a remarkable impression of a gnarler, barking an alarm. "I don't 'old with no man treating 'is mistress bad."

"No! Nay!" Thea's companion practically shouted in her determination to defend her mate (a good sign, Thea thought). "Nothing such as that, I prom-ise. Losing patience with me...sexually"—Lady Eliz-abeth whispered the last word as though to speak it at full volume might tarnish her tongue—"not phys-ically. 'Tis simply that I don't want him turning else-where for carnal companionship, not if I can help it."

Reassured, Susan gulped her tea down to porce-lain. With a clack, she returned her cup to its saucer; a clatter and the saucer met the tray. "Can't make no guarantees you understand, men will be men, but I believe I can help you out much as anyone could."

"Thank heavens." Lady Elizabeth placed her untouched tea silently on the tray. "Please, share whatever you will."

"To keep him from *wanting* to stray, you must convince him how much you like havin' *carnal* rela-tions with him." Susan latched on to the phrase with a twinkle. "Now some gents are going to ply their plow in multiple pastures no matter how hard you try to lock the gate, but if yours asked *you* to be his mistress, why 'tis obvious that priggin' others ain't in his plans."

"Ah-ah," Thea interjected when she heard Lady Elizabeth choke back a gasp. "Mayhap 'prigging' isn't the best term to use in this situation. Have you another descriptor?"

"His tiller doesn't seek to venture into other pastures, aye? 'E's content with planting fields close to home. 'Ow's that?"

Though she thought perhaps Susan was getting her nautical ships, garden plots and masculine shafts confused, Thea didn't have the heart to correct her, not again. "I think we can all agree that to be a correct assumption."

"But *how* do I prevent pasture straying or his tiller drifting elsewhere?" Lady Elizabeth cried in a frustrated tone. "I've no notion at all. No understanding of what he *expects* of me. Especially when more experienced fields lie *everywhere*."

"Don't let that bother you none. 'Experienced' might just mean more practiced at falsifying whether he's any good at it."

"I don't quite grasp your meaning."

As though it were knowledge *everyone* possessed, Susan explained, "*Pretending*, Lady Wylde. Really good mistresses know how to feign it with conviction."

"Feign what?"

"How much you're enjoying their cock in your cu—"

"Susan!" Thea gave her head a sharp shake, indicating *that* particular language was well beyond the pale.

Nodding sagely, Susan corrected herself. "Enjoying their penis in your privates." She glanced at Thea, gauging the suitability of her substitution.

Thea smiled her approval, barely masking a very unladylike laugh.

This was delightful. Horrible that Lady Elizabeth felt the need for such assistance, but a positive delight that Thea was, remarkably, in a position to provide education, even in a roundabout way.

And if she happened to benefit from today's lesson? Well then, all the better.

"All right then," Lady Elizabeth said decisively. "Teach me how to fake it. I shall endeavor to be the most convincing mistress in all of England!"

"Wait." That plan troubled Thea. "Does this mean you *don't* enjoy, ah...feeling Lord Wylde *there*?" she managed to ask without putting herself to too terrible a blush.

Lady Elizabeth's gaze bounced around the room while she answered. "I thought I did. Enjoyed it, that is. Or at least I believe I was coming to but then— Well..."

When she trailed off and showed no signs of continuing, Susan took over. "Lady Wylde?"

Red as a cherry, Lady Elizabeth looked back at Susan. "Aye?"

"I believe mayhap we're comin' at this from the wrong side."

"How do you mean?"

Susan thought for a moment. Then she toed off her slippers, brought her legs to the chair beneath her voluminous skirts and leaned forward, elbows to her knees. Looking anything but a mistress, she proposed, "Let's start over with *your* expectations, shall we? With how you're approachin' his, ah...er, *plowing*."

At her hesitant nod, Susan continued. "If you like his aspects, that helps."

"His aspects?" Lady Elizabeth seemed as perplexed as Thea.

"Aye. His manly aspects, the ones beneath his breeches." When that brought no response, Susan pierced Lady Elizabeth with a blunt look. "Do you like the way 'e looks naked?"

Oh, yes, Thea couldn't help but think the answer, picturing Lord Tremayne.

"I, ahm...I..." Lady Elizabeth was having more difficulty it seemed.

"You *have* seen him in the buff, haven't you?" Susan persisted.

"I've—I've seen parts of him without clothing."

"Parts, eh? The parts you've seen, then." Susan was starting to sound exasperated. "'E's your husband and all you've seen are *parts*? Never mind, tell me—when you consider his various naked parts, do you find you want to see more?"

Every time we're together.

Lady Elizabeth's answer was to turn scarlet. And not say a word.

"His face," Susan said patiently, trying another tack, "do you like his face?"

Very much.

"Very much so."

Thea smiled.

"That's real good. How about I make it easy," Susan suggested, "give you a short list of things to work on?"

"That sounds grand. Proceed."

Ticking them off on her fingers, Susan began with gusto. "One, you cannot be afraid to show 'im what you like. Two—"

"But how?" Lady Elizabeth interrupted.

"By touchin' yourself while he watches." Susan admirably ignored the strangling sounds coming from the couch. "There's other ways but that's the easiest. Two, if it feels good, 'ave—*have*—fun with it. You ain't hurting nobody and who cares what the law says?"

The law?

"Three, make sure you..."

IN THE END, the Dreaded Speech was a near disaster but not a total one. Not from Daniel's viewpoint.

Penry never made it. Daniel found out later another marriage proposal for his second eldest, which resulted in jealous sisters and an elated and effusively talkative wife, delayed him. That and an untimely carriage-wheel mishap conspired to keep him far away from the committee meeting. By the time he finally showed, everyone else had gone home.

Wylde, on the other hand, at least put in an appearance. Pity it was half an hour too late.

The votes had already been tallied, the buffoon arses on the other side of the table unwilling to wait or reschedule before moving for a vote, with his brother-in-law's side coming up three short. So even had both men been present, Wylde still would have gone home disappointed. Although "disappointed" wasn't quite how the man looked... Daniel couldn't tell if that was bashfulness or brazenness filling his friend's distracted gaze, but something was definitely off. Given how intently the man had lobbied for a different outcome, his lack of anger over the result made less sense than a goat with two heads.

As for Daniel's mouth, it stammered and muttered through, hampered by the absence of its two promised and most stalwart supporters, but hearkened by his own revelation: he really didn't give a damn what these men thought about him.

In the last couple of days, he'd realized only the opinions of those *he* truly valued meant a whit. Wylde, Penry, Ellie of course. Thea (went without saying). Even Everson and Tom—possibly especially these two—had all conspired to bring the truth home: he couldn't change what was. He couldn't control how others responded or viewed him. But he could choose his friends and how he dealt with them.

He could focus his efforts on spending more time with those he liked and respected, and his energies in the direction of broadening a few more horizons. After the entertaining hours spent with the Eversons yesterday and the surprisingly pleasurable evening at the opera—with mistress *and* family—Daniel was no longer content to squirrel his life away and himself in a dark corner. No longer agreeable to avoiding every possible conversation.

But now, instead of looking forward to Thea's, at turns soothing and scintillating, company, he was expected to remain home tonight—alone? For some deuced surprise Ellie had concocted?

Devil take him!

What was the world coming to when a man had to moderate his blazing passions at the request of his *mistress*?

3

PLANETARY – AND OTHER – BODIES COLLIDE

"AH, MRS. HURWELL." Mr. Taft greeted Thea with a warm and relieved expression that evening moments after her clock *dinged* ten times. Refusing to remove his raindrop-speckled greatcoat, he addressed her from just inside the door. "I despaired over finding you at home and receiving, but I only now arrived at the hotel and was informed of your letter. Thank goodness you included your direction. I'm leaving for home early tomorrow—it's my grandson's tenth birthday. Can't miss that, now could I?"

"Of course not," she said automatically, glancing at Buttons who'd let in the renowned clockmaker as Mr. and Mrs. Samuels had already retired.

Upon returning from her excursion with Lady Wylde, Thea had indulged in a thorough washing and donned one of the new ensembles Madame V had graciously delivered while Thea was out.

The dressmaker had sent round two simple day dresses, both cut down from ones she'd brought the day before, along with matching slippers. The message accompanying the package instructed Thea to present herself Monday morning for fittings on several others.

This gown was much more to her liking than the fancy, false-fronted one of last evening. In the Grecian style, caught up beneath her breasts with a jade ribbon, the pastel green cambric trimmed with a single layer of ecru lace pleased her immensely.

In it, she actually *felt* like a real lady for once, which was the only reason she was still up and attired when her late-evening visitor came calling.

But as Mr. Taft finished his smiling greeting— after expressing his pleasure at seeing her again and his regret at needing to leave at first light—he baffled her thoroughly with his next words. "If you're agreeable and think he won't be overly inconvenienced by the hour, don your winter gear and we'll go visit your Lord Tremayne and see if we can fix his orrery right up."

We? "Now?"

"Of course, my dear. You don't expect me to call upon the man without your chaperonage?" He laughed good-naturedly. "A little above my station, wouldn't you say? But I'm pleased as a pickle to see you've picked up such a lofty suitor. Hate to hear Hurwell's gone but glad you've moved on."

He thought Lord Tremayne was courting her?

Well, shear her like a Suffolk sheep!

Couldn't he tell? That in truth she was Lord Tremayne's kept woman? His strumpet?

Her panicked gaze flicked to the nude portraits. But they were gone, replaced by a waterfall on one side and a close-up of songbirds on the other. Knowing she'd just heard clocks chime, she looked for the sinfully suggestive cuckoo, but the wall was blank. The figurines were missing as well, the only thing gracing her crimson table runner was the silver tray and a vase of fresh, peppy flowers.

Startled, she turned to Buttons, who still stood unobtrusively to one side. Noticing what she was about (no doubt aided by her levitating eyebrows), he pointed directly overhead. *Master chamber* he mouthed and her heart rate settled down from its rapid-fire pace.

Courting me? Thea mouthed back because it seemed as good a way to communicate as any. Buttons shrugged, then nodded, as though uncertain how to correct the erroneous assumption but still offering both support and encouragement.

When the clockmaker again urged her toward the door, Thea finally acquiesced.

It looked as though she and Mr. Taft would be paying her protector a call. Thea forbore from calling on the Almighty to deliver her from this mess. She'd made her naughty bed and enjoyed rolling around in it; now wasn't the time to turn squeamish.

. . .

IN MOMENTS, they were rolling swiftly through the wet streets, the jagged lightning in the distance protesting her subterfuge. Buttons had squeezed in next to the driver after whispering to Thea that he'd try to make sure "his lordship got the drift of things".

While Mr. Taft reminisced fondly of his past trips to London and Thea answered appropriately if distractedly, one thought kept her seated and not running for the sanctuary of her just-departed town-house: she'd learned from Lord Tremayne's sister that he wasn't married.

Thank God and chatty relations for that tidbit. It was one thing to show up on his doorstep; quite another to be confronted with his unsuspecting, betrayed wife.

BORED WITH EVERYTHING he'd tried (obsessed with his new mistress, more like) Daniel decided to retire at half past ten.

In his shirtsleeves after more tinkering with one of his working orreries, ironically *slowing* the rotation of Uranus on this particular specimen (darn planet put all the others to shame with its snail's crawl of an eighty-plus year orbit of the Sun), he was just leaving his study and approaching the stairs that led up to his bedchamber when the door knocker clanged.

Who would be calling at this hour?

Frowning, he started down the stairs instead.

He'd ordered Rumsley to bed when he found out his butler's gout was acting up again. John had stepped out with Ellie's maid a while ago, after seeing whether Daniel needed anything or wanted him to remain on duty. He'd sent his footman off with his blessing. At least one of them could be with their lady tonight.

The door knocker banged again, and he descended the last few treads at a run before his quiet household was further disturbed by the racket.

He swung the heavy door wide and about choked on his own spit. Surprise warred with astonishment.

"Thea!" On his doorstep and with some spry, grey-haired fellow.

Thea, the guilt in her eyes not enough to temper his pleasure at seeing her. Despite the stormy night, she fairly sparkled in the pelisse he'd given her. Thea was right—the sleeves were overly long. She worried one with several bare fingers while her other hand simply trembled, her arm crooked around that of her companion.

"Thea," he said again, dumbly. Numbly. What was she doing here? At his home? And why did the notion, instead of annoying him as it certainly would have with Good-Riddance-Former Mistress, only seem perfect because it was Thea?

"Mrs. Hurwell?" The elderly fellow smiled at them both. "Is this your Lord Tremayne? And answering his own door?"

Mrs. Hurwell?

It sounded all wrong. How he'd started to hate that name. It wasn't right, not at all.

It should be Mrs. Holbrook, Lady Tremayne.

His lady. And he should swell her trim belly with child.

A child they'd both love whether he or she stammered or whistled or came out plaid.

"My lord." She raised one hand as though to ward him off and Daniel shook himself free of the fantasy with a strangled sound. When had all the air evaporated from his entryway?

"Please forgive our late and unannounced arrival," she began, and shot a worried look over her shoulder. A flash of lightning illuminated Swift John hovering protectively behind her. "This is Mr. Taft. I was given to understand you desired to hear him speak but that your favor for Lord Wylde prevented it."

At the introduction, the other man leaned forward and caught sight of Daniel's bruised phiz (Ellie had yet to deliver that requested batch of cream). "My gracious, my lord. I do hope the other fellow looks worse."

"Lord Tremayne is a pugilist," Thea explained to her companion while somehow managing to shoot Daniel a private glare that would have smote a lesser man than he. But still, he heard the pride in her voice as she defended him.

Him! For childishly fighting to avoid the demons of his past.

Was she an angel, perhaps? An angel

masquerading as a mistress? One sent to rescue him from all his demons?

Her subdued voice went on, something about timing and birthdays, but all Daniel heard were her lilting tones. All he saw was the woman never far from his thoughts. All he wanted was to snatch her up and escape with her to his chambers.

As the man beside her chimed in, Daniel finally grasped all they were saying.

This was Mr. Taft, famed orrery expert, who had somehow concluded that Daniel was a suitor for the hand of his mistress. Which would be comical if it wasn't so close to the truth.

Which also explained why Thea looked so miserably guilty and kept trying to edge back. (If it wasn't for Taft's fatherly patting of her hand upon his forearm, she might have succeeded.)

Mr. Taft, offering to help fix Daniel's machine. The very machine his grandfather had consulted with Taft about back in the 1770s.

This was Ellie's surprise?

And it brought Thea to his doorstep?

More than a bit in awe of the older man, never mind that he resembled a grinning, grey-tufted elf, Daniel felt his jaw tightening characteristically. Manners bade he recall himself sufficiently to usher them in.

"P-please," he cleared his throat, praying they hadn't noticed the slip, "come in, b-both of you."

Damn! Was it nerves that made it so bad? Taft's presence? Or Thea's? Or was he simply overly tired after the disappointing showing at the committee meeting?

Taft was waiting for Thea to precede him, but like a giant, unmovable oak, she appeared rooted in place.

"Thea?" Daniel stepped outside and forcibly shepherded her across the threshold. She gave him a grateful look. Weighted with more guilt.

Using the excuse of helping her with her pelisse, he whispered in her ear. "'Tis fine, really. I'm—" *Pleased. Delighted. Blighted by your beauty.* "Stay with my—blsng." *Blessing* got smothered against her nape when he took advantage of the situation to press his lips to her soft, sweet skin. To inhale her unique and calming fragrance. Essence of Thea.

When his lips lingered, he swore she gave a silent moan and leaned into him. Then she nodded, straightening as she pulled her arm from the long sleeve, only to reveal a delightful new dress. He smiled his approval, reluctant to release her, but beyond curious about this unforeseen visit.

AFTER LORD TREMAYNE asked a single question about that afternoon's lecture he'd missed, which started Mr. Taft on a whirlwind of excited explanations, the men headed up the staircase.

Buttons nudged Thea.

She left off staring at the opulent chandelier overhead. "Aye?"

"Go on with you," Buttons told her in a low voice.

"Look there—" He nodded toward the stairs. "His lordship's waiting for you."

He was, standing stalwart and strong, gaze intense, hand outstretched. And that's when she noticed his attire. Clothed the most casually she'd ever seen him—save for in her bedchamber—his thick hair was finger-tousled, linen shirt billowing and dark breeches thigh-hugging. No tailcoat. No waistcoat. Neckcloth loose, practically cast aside.

Though he stood there, beckoning to her, she had the uncanny feeling the tiled marble floor she stood on was flinging energy spikes through her slippers and straight up her legs, spikes that loudly proclaimed *You don't belong here. You don't belong!*

Lord Tremayne's townhouse put hers to shame. Everything around her exuded tasteful elegance on the grandest of scales. This townhouse could swallow her entire abode several times over—and that was just for the appetizer.

But it was the man himself who created the longing to stay.

The man with the discolored face and charming smile, the broad shoulders subdued by nothing more than quality linen. The man whose quiet but decisively spoken, "Thea?" tamed those condemning floor spikes into ones of *Welcome*.

The motion concealed by her long dress, she stamped her feet. Yet still, it came again: *Welcome*.

Flashing Buttons a grateful smile, she climbed the stairs after them, glad more than ever for her new dress when Lord Tremayne took stock of it and nodded as she came abreast. "Lovely."

That was all he said. But 'twas enough to have her heart galloping in response. She could repent or regret tomorrow; tonight she intended to collect every glimpse of the inner man Lord Tremayne deigned to share.

"'TIS A BEAUTY!" Mr. Taft exclaimed upon entering the study, going unerringly to the largest orrery in the room. Five or six feet across, it was easily higher than her waist. By far the biggest one Thea had encountered, all of her previous experience being with the miniature clock-top models and an occasional tabletop orrery.

"I'd seen the plans on her," Mr. Taft continued, "but not the finished apparatus. She fulfilled her design and then some. What seems to be the problem with her, my lord?"

"Uranus," Lord Tremayne said succinctly, following Mr. Taft over to the piece while she remained just inside the open door, ready for a quick escape should one prove necessary. "Refuses to or...bit."

"Well then, it's our duty to practitioners of astrolatry everywhere to get her running smoothly, is it not?" While Mr. Taft reached the device and started evaluating the individual planets and parts as he might a hotly desired horse at auction, she worked to puzzle out the meaning of the unfamiliar word. *Astro* was easy: celestial or heavenly bodies. *Latry* had her stumped, until with a mental snap she recalled idolatry and quickly deduced Mr. Taft referenced enthusiastic sky-watchers, worshipers of heavenly objects.

After investigating the orrery's perimeter, he bent to peer into the central shaft where all the planetary orbits originated. "Have you trouble with any others? Or do they all run like clockwork, heh?"

Lord Tremayne smiled at his jest. "Just Uranus. B-b—" He coughed into his hand. "Finished in seventy-eight, you see."

"Ah. That explains it."

Explains what? Thea wanted to venture but was hesitant to speak, hesitant to draw attention to herself. No matter what his eyes and actions conveyed, breaching the home of one's protector was ill-advised—if not an outright hanging offense. *The Mistress Code of Expected Behavior* Susan and Lady Wylde planned to pen was surely catching fire at Thea's brazenness.

Seeing a yawning dog emerge from beneath a huge mahogany desk, she relinquished her post to make her way to one of the large chairs near it. She perched on the edge but the leather was so very comfortable, she found herself sinking right in. She held out her hand and was rewarded when the big canine sniffingly advanced.

"You must be Cyclops, hmmm, boy?" she whispered to the ugliest dog she'd ever seen, one eye vacant, muzzle scarred and askew, drool drizzling from one side of his jaw. Nevertheless, there was something endearing in the way he nuzzled her thigh and pushed his head under her hand, not content until she was scratching everywhere she could reach.

When she approached the underside of his chin, she swore the dog purred. She giggled to herself. He angled his head and gave a happy, slobbering bark, and Thea couldn't help but cringe when she noticed they'd unintentionally captured the men's attention.

So she braved speaking up. "What does seventy-eight explain?"

"Uranus was discovered in 1781, a handful of years after this beauty was built," Mr. Taft told her, arms wide as though he'd hug the huge, broken contraption if he could. "Thought it was a comet at first, but the scientists of the day soon put that to rights. I can just imagine after all the effort put into this darling how its creator would be vexed beyond reckoning to miss out on the greatest astronomical discovery in his lifetime."

When she nodded with interest, he continued, his enthusiasm for his topic growing. "The planets through Saturn were discovered back in ancient times, you see. For centuries, nothing so exciting has been identified so conclusively. And now she has us to set her to rights!" Taft fairly glowed at the challenge.

"Aye," Lord Tremayne confirmed, touching a

gentle fingertip to the bright blue ball representing Uranus.

A faraway look came into his eyes as he skimmed his fingers over the longest arm. The light touch was at odds with the hardness she glimpsed in his flexing jaw, the growing tension she sensed emanating from him. Perhaps he realized the absurdity of having his mistress occupy his study, and with a witness he so obviously respected?

She shifted, tempted to flee all over again. But just then Cyclops closed his eye and sighed, nestling his head heavily upon her lap.

"WAS ADDED THEN," Daniel forced out. "Worked." His bloody neck was starting to seize up on him. He wanted to howl, or at least curse his blighted mouth. Instead he ungritted his teeth and tried to explain. "Then stored. A-b-bu-*bandoned*."

Son of a bitch!

"Difficulty getting the words out, my lord? Just take your time." Smiling serenely, the man gave Thea an understanding look during this little speech —the speech that threatened to destroy Daniel's composure if not his life. "I'm in no hurry, not when in the company of such a magnificent specimen and people who appreciate her."

While Daniel felt his world tilt on its axis, sensed more than saw the rigidity that came into Thea's posture, the way she quickly turned from stroking Cy to studying them, Taft blithely carried on. "My uncle was the same way. Got tripped up by stubborn letters now and then..."

Goddammit, why now? Just when he'd started to believe *he* could tell her, could admit his weakness and it might not condemn him back to silence, might not mean the immediate end of what they shared.

But he'd thought to tell her *his* way, in his own time. Perhaps next month, after getting her bosky on fine brandy or sauced on wine. Or next year, after getting her with child—

Good God? Where had that come from? On the heels of his earlier thoughts too. Damn him. Twice in one night he thought to impregnate her?

A child wasn't a pawn. Wasn't, in truth, anything he'd ever thought about before, not in relation to *his* fathering one. But he imagined it *now*? When the sun had exploded and blackness crashed in around him?

Nay, he only sought to hold on to the woman he loved, to keep her by his side—and in the dark about his defect—a little (or a lot) longer.

Daniel didn't have to look at Thea to see how still she'd gone. How alert. How her eyes no doubt narrowed with suspicion when all he could do was keep his gaze fixed on the planet he no longer saw and jerk a nod, agreeing with his idol that he was a clodpated ninnyhammer.

His hand slipped. The gears pinched, then severed his skin. "D-damn."

Hah. How the universe mocked and laughed. He couldn't even get that out, a single swearword?

Couldn't even split his finger and drip blood on his precious orrery without becoming a stammering fool?

"Got you, eh?" Taft commiserated as Daniel whipped out a handkerchief and wrapped it around his finger. Taft was already blotting the crimson smear off the brass. "No matter how much I profess to love them, these orrery rascals have a way of biting back, especially the worthwhile ones."

"Aye." It came out a curse.

"It was the same for my uncle," Taft went on, oblivious to the interstellar explosion he'd just set off in Daniel's stomach. "Hated having to talk in public or meet new people."

And that did it. Nailed him in his coffin as surely as an undertaker. But Taft wasn't finished yet. 'Course not. He just wanted to dig those nails in a little deeper. "Probably why he was so good with mechanics. Screws and such don't talk back, eh, my lord?" He followed up this pithy pronouncement with a heartfelt sigh. "He's the one who fostered my interest in clockworks and orreries, you know. Smartest man I ever knew, my uncle. Miss him terribly."

Smartest man he knew?

There was that, at least.

Daniel had two choices: halt their efforts and deal with Thea—assuming she stayed long enough to let him—or carry on with the plaguingly perceptive man who had troubled himself to come lend aid.

What he refused to do was run away. Hide from the truth any longer, no matter how nauseous he felt, now that it was out.

Breathing through his nose with every bit of control he could exert, Daniel told himself this was his house, his study, his broken orrery, his mistress... Oh God, it was his *everything*. In vain he tried to muster courage where none existed. A fruitless effort. It had fled.

But he refused to let his mind do the same. There would be no pretending this wasn't happening, no cloud-hopping escape to avoid the pain of the whip. Nay, it was time he took a stand. Brave whatever censure might come his way without hiding in the corner as he'd been taught by the lash.

Though it took more nerve than stepping into a ring with the beefiest of opponents, Daniel broke free from the coffin and nailed his feet in place. He swallowed twice, still without looking at Thea. "For me, 't-twas my grandfather."

"Your grandfather, eh?"

"Aye. T-teaching me of orreries."

Taft nodded, pulled a magnifying glass from his pocket and bent closer. "Some say they're a waste of money and one's crown office." The man sniffed as though *those* people were the idiots, not smart ones like his uncle. Like Daniel. He nudged Daniel with an elbow. "But we'll show up their ignorant hides, eh? Get this sweetheart running..."

· · ·

LORD TREMAYNE HAD TROUBLE SPEAKING?

Thea had forgotten to inhale. When her lungs protested, she came to with a slight choke. One she quickly muffled behind her hand, unable to stop staring at the men whose heads were bent over Uranus's arm, inspecting it from bright-blue ball to innermost gear.

After seven-plus long years with Mr. Hurwell, she'd learned to hold her tongue. She did so now, working through what it all meant.

Lord Tremayne had trouble speaking.

Which explained so much, did it not?

Why he tended to arrive later than expected; it minimized talking opportunities if he was always rushing into place at the last second.

Why their flirty letters flowed with an ease, a verbosity she'd noticed on more than one occasion was absent from their in-person interactions.

Why he spoke so very deliberately, unless they were already laughing and the mirth masked the stammer for him.

Why he never came for dinner. Never lingered once they were intimate.

Has he told you anything more? Lady Elizabeth had asked at the opera. *About himself?*

Her mind whirled, remembering stutters and stumbles she'd overlooked or deemed unimportant at the time, given the wondrous topics they'd discussed. Remembering the ticking jaw or gritted teeth, the strained tendons in his neck that usually gave way to a brief word or two. Remembering the bruises he sported, both old and new.

So, this explained his reserve, his inclination toward tardiness. Did it explain the fighting? She'd have to work on that one.

When she didn't feel so slighted.

At the moment Thea struggled with resentment. Waves of it clogging her throat, knotting her belly. It was a simple enough difficulty to explain. Why hadn't he told her? Did he not trust her?

Oh, he trusted her with his body but not with who he was. And that hurt. Made her feel as though his lack of trust was somehow *her* fault.

But she hadn't missed how his free hand had clutched the table with a white-knuckled grip. Nor had she missed how his spine had gone stiff, his ears slightly red. How his gaze studiously avoided hers.

He knew she'd overheard. Knew his secret was out. And the information affected him mightily.

Thea chose to stay where she was. Hadn't her mother taught her that actions conveyed more of a person's character than what they said?

Thoughtful gifts, joyous letters, a safe home, friendly servants...

Cyclops huffed, upset when she stopped petting, so she applied herself to making it up to him, never mind the growing damp patch on her dress.

Stray twins (thieves, no less), fearsome, drooly dogs (but lovable for all that)...and now her? It appeared Lord Tremayne had a propensity for rescuing those in need. Thea wasn't quite sure what to make of her new philanthropic protector.

Was she just another in a long line of strays?

A few minutes later, after pulling out several intricate-looking tools from a rolled pouch he carried on his person, Mr. Taft called across the room. "Mrs. Hurwell, can you come over here, if you would? This part here needs a woman's delicate touch and smaller fingers."

"Certainly." She transferred Cyclops's muzzle to the chair and stood without meeting Lord Tremayne's gaze. There was too much unsaid between them, too many emotions roiling through her (and she couldn't even begin to fathom what *he* must be feeling). Nay, when she stared into his eyes again, they needed to be alone.

So she walked forward as normally as she could manage, keeping her gaze trained on the stately contraption. Though the room seemed to swirl and spin around her, the walls coming closer, then receding at once, the giant orrery remained a touchstone.

Lord Tremayne blurred as she approached, the floor beneath her feet pitched as though they were at sea. But the orrery stayed in sharp focus. Uranus wasn't a mere blue ball, she realized as she fought the strange sensations and closed the distance. It was a perfectly spherical carving from lapis lazuli.

How beautiful. How...ordinary.

When her entire world just kept whirling.

Whirling. Like that dratted planet needed to, in order to please the man who'd given her so much.

When she reached the intimidating apparatus, she skirted round it and came up directly between the two gentlemen.

Where she reached out and found Lord Tremayne's arm. He was no longer hazy; no longer blurry. He was solid strength and quiet, gentle power. Safety *and* seduction.

He was the best thing she'd ever come into contact with, and she wasn't about to give him up.

She slid her fingers down his shirtsleeve until she could slip her hand into his. Without their audience being aware, she gave a light squeeze, mindful of the handkerchief wrapped around the cut finger, telling him without words that *she* wouldn't be the one to abandon what they'd started.

Only when Mr. Taft spoke again did she reluctantly release her hold.

"Right here." Mr. Taft indicated where he needed her assistance. "If you could just…"

***

AN HOUR LATER, after they'd finally coaxed Uranus to rotate as it should, in proper concert with the other six planets, and very aware of Thea's gaze boring into his back, Daniel escorted Taft out of his study.

All things considered, it had been a tolerably successful evening.

In addition to his grandfather's orrery, the three

of them had also tweaked another one where Jupiter insisted on circling too fast (actually, Thea had nimbly adjusted the mechanism—after she'd wound them all up for Taft's enjoyment—while the two men looked on).

Imagine that—a mechanically minded female.

Imagine that—his childhood idol exposing his secret sins to that very female.

Imagine his surprise when she *hadn't* stared at him with derision or ridicule. No pity or sympathy either.

Just unwavering, silent support. Daniel hadn't—

"Lord Tremayne, you must forgive an old fool usually surrounded by family and used to flapping his jaws at the least provocation."

Barely three steps down the stairway, Taft launched into the most effusive of apologies. "It became apparent to me as the night wore on I'd veritably stepped in it. Oh, she tried to cover it, but 'twas obvious you'd not yet let on to Mrs. Hurwell about the speaking hesitations. Amazing, really, that you mask it so well. To get close enough to court a woman without her knowing—

"But that's neither here nor there." Upon reaching the entry, Taft stopped to draw on his coat, piercing Daniel with a sincere look of regret. "I humbly beg your forgiveness for letting my tongue tread where it had no business."

Before Daniel could grant absolution and proffer his sincere thanks for all they'd accomplished, the man clamped his hat on his head and clapped his hands together. "Well now, seeing your collection has proved the pinnacle of my London jaunt. That and seeing Mrs. Hurwell so happy. Do please give her a chance, my lord. With the truth I mean. She's both kind and resourceful. Wouldn't have said so in her presence, but I always thought she was wasted on ol' Hurwell. Bit of a curmudgeondy fellow if you ask me."

"I agree," Daniel got out before Taft nodded politely and exited, Swift John overly eager to summon the carriage that would return the clockmaker to his hotel.

That was fast.

Just then his housekeeper bundled by. Catching sight of him, Mrs. Peterson paused with a smile and open look of inquiry. *Is there anything I can do for you?* her kindly face asked.

The woman couldn't hear a lick, which had always suited Daniel just fine. She read lips and gestures remarkably well. So it was easy to retrieve Thea's pelisse, point to a spot on the sleeve, and make a motion with his fingers. With a nod, Mrs. Peterson bustled off, pelisse in hand.

Swift John stomped back in, wiping his wet feet on the rug. "Nice gent," his footman commented, smoothing down the ever-present cowlick with a rain-slicked hand. "Friendly sort."

Daniel grunted.

What now?

Taft was gone. *But Thea isn't.*

The air expelled from his lungs so hard they ached.

"Well?" Swift John damn near clicked his heels together.

Daniel glared.

His servant ignored him and stared up the staircase, gaze fixed in the direction of Daniel's study. "So, your lordship, she's up there, is our Miss Thea..."

Our Miss Thea?

What? It wasn't enough he'd not been alone with her all day; now he was expected to share her with his servants?

Something rather akin to a growl surfaced from the depths of his chest.

The impudent servant only grinned. "Aye, up there. In *your* study. All alone. *Waiting. Fer. You.*"

Swift John couldn't have yelled *Get your cowardly arse up there!* any louder.

Where was a good opera when one needed to escape?

4

WHEREUPON THE MISTRESS
BECOMES THE MASTER

Once the mistress masters masterpieces her masterful master masterfully teaches, she manifests these mastered expertises upon his masterful centerpiece with eager reaches!

Kamasutra (as translated by Thomas Edward Everson into *Adoring Arts of Luscious Love*, circa 1830s)

THEA WASN'T QUITE sure how Mr. Taft arranged it, but he'd managed to depart—alone. *Without her!*

Oh, he'd clasped his hands to both of hers, eyes twinkling, as he expressed his delight in seeing her again ("and with you looking so radiant!"), and he'd more reservedly shaken Lord Tremayne's hand and glowed over the shared challenge—and its successful outcome...

But then he'd rendered *her* speechless when he'd secured Lord Tremayne's escort downstairs so he could take his leave after giving Thea a silent but emphatic command to stay put and see things made right, this expressed through the most regretful, and thoughtful, of looks.

Well, surprise her to Southampton and back, but she was starting to think the orrery expert was something of a magician as well. How else to explain her presence—after midnight—in the home of her beloved if bullheaded protector?

"That... Wasn't..." Lord Tremayne came through the open doorway already speaking. "Wasn't..." He stopped far away from where she tinkered with another beautiful specimen, this one more of a fantasy, showing comets and nebulae and all sorts of celestial wonders orbiting their double suns, with nary a planet in sight. Straightening, she faced him and waited.

His breath heaved from him like lava bursting from a volcano. "Find...out."

His jaw was granite, eyes like steel. His hands kept flexing into fists at his sides.

He stood there holding her gaze—the self-loathing so evident in his, she thought her heart would crack.

Despite the heaviness centered in her stomach, the fear he'd push her away now that she knew, now that they were alone, her feet suddenly sprouted wings. She rushed to him and only stopped when he put a hand out as though warding her off.

"Just say it, please," she implored, "without taxing yourself so. Whatever you think to express."

DANIEL CLOSED his eyes against the appeal in hers. "I...can...not."

"But you can with me! The difficulty you have doesn't diminish you in my eyes." Her voice grew softer even as it strengthened. She touched his arm. "Don't you see by now? Nothing could."

At that, his eyelids flew open. "I..."

Her fingers tightened on his wrist. "Except perhaps if you persist in fighting to the point your face looks like a field of wildflowers."

She sounded so like Ellie, he tried to smile. "Thea. I... I—" Tension clawed up his neck and sank talons into his throat.

Penry's morning call, the afternoon speech, utter surprise at his late-evening visitors. *Talking* with Taft the last hour. Exposing his affliction to Thea, unable to hide or avoid speaking...

He was hurting now, every bit as much as after Everson's yesterday. Mayhap more. Scraped raw, swollen, ravaged by invisible arrows—Cupid's damn arrow—he knew not which. Likely everything.

The pain was so great, if it hadn't been for all those years inuring himself against his brother's taunts, his father's beatings, Daniel would've broken down and wept.

Not an option!

He swore and broke away from Thea, marched to

the first solid surface he saw—the side of a book-case, and slammed his hand against it.

He needed distance. Needed to escape.

But he didn't *want* to.

His stinging palm hit the bookcase again as he willed his throat and neck to stop clenching. Stop punishing him.

"Stop." Thea echoed his thoughts, feathering her fingers over his jaw, his cheeks. "Stop. You've done enough for one day. I can see the strain in your neck, the fatigue in your eyes. Tomorrow is soon enough. You can explain then, all you want, and I'll gladly listen. Or later still, next week. Next month, even; I care not which. You need to rest."

She wrapped her hands around his abused one and started tugging him toward the door. "Now, Buttons is here and *could* take me home or *you* could take me to your bedchamber— Ah-ah," she admonished when he started to say something. She was making this too easy for him. "Tonight, I talk for the both of us. Personally, I would just as soon stay here. In your bed, of course. But I'm fully aware how vastly inappropriate—"

"There's nn-*no* mirror," exploded unbidden.

Color mantled her cheeks when she smiled. "Silly man," she spoke to his nicked finger, softly touching the injured spot. "I don't need a mirror to love you."

He couldn't contemplate whether she meant it literally, not now. Not when he needed to hold her so damn bad. Needed to bury his lips against the sweet skin of her neck and forget what a buffoon he'd made of himself the last hour.

With a growl loud enough to be heard in the kitchens, Daniel swung her into his arms and barreled through the doorway.

One look and a hovering Buttons was nodding—his bit-upon lips unable to stifle his grin—and running down the stairs, in the opposite direction, saying, "Aye, milord, you have it. I'll see the team gets stabled for the night and get word to Sam and his missus so they don't worry none about Miss Thea. See you in the morning an' not before!"

"How grand," Thea enthused, tucking her face in the crook of his neck as he turned toward the stairs. Up close, his divine scent could have crumbled her to her knees. Good thing he carried her.

Warming her lips against his fragrant skin, she said, "It appears as though we get to be inappropriate together." She caressed the thick hair at his nape, threading her fingers through the cool, silken strands. She couldn't help but notice the muscles of his neck beneath. "And look, you're so strong, I don't even need to hold on."

Joyfully, she kicked her feet and waved her arms as he ascended the steps. He didn't make so much as a perceptible pause. "No doubt I could roll over and try my hand at archery and you'd still hold tight."

He muttered something that sounded suspiciously like, "God save me."

"Nuh-uh, my lord," she chided gently when he reached the bedroom—not breathing a speck harder than usual—and swung her to her feet. If she entertained him sufficiently by rattling her own jaws, perhaps 'twould keep him from worrying his. "Do you forget so soon? I'm charged with all the talking tonight. You may reciprocate another time."

Not giving him leave to protest—or herself a chance to inspect his chamber, she set about the smile-worthy task of ridding them of their clothes.

A light push to his chest and she backed him to the bed. A single finger to his shoulder and he sat.

"Boots." She pointed. "Off. Now." She giggled. (Giggled? Definitely not something she'd done much of in her past.) "See? I can say a lot in a few words too."

As she stepped back to give him room, he snared her waist and hauled her to him. Slanting her mouth downward with a strong hand to the back of her head, he captured her gasp of surprise and gave her a bruisingly fierce kiss.

The pressure of his mouth upon hers said so much.

With bold sweeps of his tongue and the firm caress of his fingers against her scalp he expressed his longing. Tender nips greeted first her top lip and then the bottom. His harsh exhalation as he scraped his teeth over the sensitive flesh he exposed when he gently sucked on her lower lip told her he'd been waiting for the right moment to devour her. To explain.

His every action shouted that he was sorry, that he cared, that he wanted her. Needed *this*. This. Whatever it was between them that defied the short amount of time they'd been together.

His hand swept down to center over one breast, to rub the slight swell, tease the nipple into an aching point. The intense pressure lifted her to her toes and into him as she toppled forward against his chest and he pulled her tongue into his mouth, as she told him, *I'm here. I need you back.*

As fast as it began, he gentled the assault. His other hand slid from her head to her spine, a sweeping caress that left tingles in its wake. The devastating kisses turned soft and romantic.

He wooed her lips into sultry surrender and the rest of her followed.

At her moan, he pulled his head back, held her gaze as his kiss-swollen mouth tilted in a not-quite smile and his palm cupped her breast even more firmly and he eased her back to her feet.

"Well now." She spoke through the passionate fog befuddling her senses. "And here you thought that would keep me quiet! Boots, sir, that's a command."

His eyes promised sensual retribution but he did as bade.

"Breeches next. Then shirt and drawers— Oh, wait!" She turned her back and scooted between his knees, thankful hers hadn't failed her—they were quivering like aspic after that swoon-worthy kiss. "Unfasten me, please? The buttons near my neck."

He did, giving her waist a deliberate squeeze before releasing her.

"Aye, I like this," she said as she untied the ribbon cinching her dress around her middle. "Like having the freedom to say whatever comes to mind without fear of being reprimanded. Mr. Hurwell was rather persnickety in that regard. Thought females didn't have the mental acumen to understand lofty topics beyond breakfast menus or starching neck-cloths." She whisked away those old concerns when she whisked her dress over her head.

"My stays? If you would, please?" Again Thea came close. "Mrs. Samuels helped me earlier—" She took a breath to give his freshly revealed chest a kiss. Backing away from his warm skin, she turned and flashed him a flirty look from over her shoulder. "I much prefer it when you help. Thank you. Your drawers now—"

When she took a step away and cast an appreciative glance over his form, the part of him protruding through the fine undergarment threatened to steal her chatter. But she was made of sterner stuff; no turning shy now! "I do realize—"

He halted her rampant ramble with an upraised finger.

"Aye?"

"Why?" He spoke without hesitating although his voice had gone completely hoarse.

"Why...?"

"Hurw..." The rough syllable sounded like a shovel scraping over stone.

Thea rushed to guess before he could harm himself further. "Why did he think me feebleminded?"

A frown crinkling his brow, Lord Tremayne shook his head.

She hazarded, "Why did I marry him?"

A relieved smile told her she'd hit upon it.

"I'll answer them both. The man had some odd notions. Thought too much contemplation on any subject would bring on a fever—mayhap that's why he was never sick? As to why I married him, my father and Mr. Hurwell were friends of long-standing—I gather he wasn't always so boorish," she confessed, shifting restlessly within her loose stays. "He'd asked me before, but I kept putting him off. When my father fell ill and urged me to accept, desperate to know I was taken care of, it seemed the most expedient way to secure his contentment before he passed."

Those horizontal lines in Lord Tremayne's fore-head grew deeper. "Mo-ther?"

"My mama? She was a lovely and warm woman who perished when I was but eleven. From good, genteel stock, or so Papa told me. She'd been finishing school and taught etiquette and how to trap—er, *secure* a rich and hopefully titled husband. Even a baronet would have sufficed, but she made the unpardonable sin of falling in love with a lowly shipping clerk, forever earning her family's animos-ity. Disowned, she was. But that was before I was born." Thea grew warm under his penetrating gaze.

"Was that a growl?" When he gave another, she stroked her fingertips down his neck. "Now I know that can't be good for your throat. Truly, Lord Tremayne, my parents were wonderful and my marriage to Mr. Hurwell wasn't *horrid*. Just horridly tedious," she assured him. "I confess, though, I'm having loads more fun with you."

He laughed at that. And gave her stays a pointed glance.

Given how he was completely bare-arsed by now, she really had no choice.

Wiggling her hips and pushing the stays down, she went back to her earlier topic, hoping the twaddle she kept spewing would cover any lingering nerves. After all, it wasn't every day she determined to seduce a gentleman.

Especially in the particular manner she *intended* to seduce him. The manner that first occurred to her after seeing the lewd and laugh-inducing cuckoo clock, the manner that beckoned even more after today's Mistress Lessons...

"I recognize I may pay for my unmitigated impertinence, taking control as I am. But alas, whether I am taken to task tomorrow or not, tonight you may not tell me 'Nay'. Not until morning light."

Fat drops of rain spattered onto the windowpane, and for the first time, she took note of the lit candles around the room, of the huge, ornate bed worthy of a king, the velvet bed hangings in a rich navy hue, the thick coverlet turned down to reveal smooth and inviting sheets. Why, the chamber appeared almost as though his servants had expected, or hoped, she'd stay the night—everything tidied and readied for seduction. Little did they know 'twas to be his!

Their surroundings bolstered her as she stepped from her stays and readied herself to remove her shift—all that remained. Hands on the bottom edge, Thea stopped to offer an apologetic look at the naked man staring at her with shining amber eyes. "One of these days—I mean nights—I do so hope to wear the extravagant night rail you gave me."

"Nnnn—" He closed his eyes as though in great pain and she didn't have the heart to chastise him, seriously or in jest. After a slow exhalation, he looked at her again. She nodded, a tiny movement meant to give encouragement or permission—or forgiveness. Mayhap all three. Whatever he needed. "Not...n-necessary."

She smiled brilliantly. "Something to anticipate, then?" He nodded and she bravely whipped off her shift. "There! Now 'tis to bed with both of us."

"Nay."

Hands to her bare hips, she frowned. "Did I not just give you orders to the contrary of expressing that particular sentiment?"

He stood, unashamed and glorious in his nakedness. Branding her with his open hand at the base of her spine, he steered her to his dresser. Upon which sat two matching boxes, each tied with a bright green ribbon. The boxes were long and slim, and when he flipped them over, she saw folded notes tucked within the ribbons.

Smiling, she reached for the one labeled *For You*. He cuffed her wrist and nudged the other box in front.

Sensation traveled up her arm. "But this one says *For Me*, which I assumed meant you." When he stroked her skin, a blaze of heat landed somewhere south of her belly. "Judging by how you're grinning, would I be correct to hazard it's for both of us?"

Open, he mouthed.

She unfolded the *For Me* note and read aloud. "*Seeing as how the other necklace is for you to wear in public—long overdue, I might add. I cannot believe I haven't sent you jewels sooner—* Really, Lord Tremayne—how you've spoiled me already! And we've only known each other, what? A week?" Thea counted backward, more surprised with every day she didn't encounter. "*Five* days. Gracious, but it seems longer, does it not?"

In answer, he pointed to where she'd left off.

"Very well," she huffed. "But I expect a full accounting of your life until this moment after you've rested." He made such a face that she laughed till her cheeks hurt. "Not exactly a prattlerate?" She nuzzled her lips to the tempting muscles on his upper chest. "I can be very persuasive, you know. Entice you to sing for me, I daresay, if the reward is sufficient."

"Read!" he barked, but his eyes were smiling. "And please, call me D-D-Daniel."

Though she saw his shoulders tense, he didn't frown at the stumble.

"I'd be honored," she answered simply, not wanting to make anything of it. If he'd just continue to open up more, he could take as long as he wanted with every word he thought to utter. "All right. Where was I?"

She scanned the page, shoring up both her spine and her voice. "All right. Here. *Sent you jewels sooner but I hope the other makes up for the recent lack. Now this one, my dear Thea*— I love it when you call me that. *This one reminds me of your beautiful n-nipples*— Ack! Now you have me doing it too!" She stared at him aghast. "I cannot believe you wrote that—"

"Thea." It was a rasp that heated her blood. "You wrote...*my* head..." His voice scratched softer and harsher over each syllable. "...*Your* lap."

"Oh. So I did. Now truly, you must rest your neck. It sounds as though you've been in a screaming contest and have drained yourself to a frazzle."

He pointed.

She read, despite the heat flushing her face with every boldly inked word slashed across the page. "*Your beautiful nipples, so bright and cherry-tipped...*"

DANIEL WAS hard-pressed not to rip the note from her hand, bend her over his dresser, and plumb her depths until she screamed his name. Until *she* went hoarse.

Primitive instincts aside, it was an easy thing to tame that urge of his. Because, by God, she was in his room, and for once, despite their nude state, despite what she was reading and the perfume of her arousal, *for once* she wasn't trembling.

Nay, she was giving voice to his words with the most dulcet of tones and it was sheer opera to his ears.

"*Cherry-tipped and so tasty I cannot wait to sup on each one*"—the rain pounded against the window in earnest and she strengthened her volume—"*with this little bauble swinging between. Wear it for me, and only me, the next time I see you. I remain, until our next night together, Yours. Daniel.*"

With endearing sentiment, she sighed and pressed his note to her chest. Right where he wanted the ruby to nestle. So he deftly slid the ribbon aside and opened the hinged box.

Overriding her gasped "*Little* bauble?" he spun her around to fasten the linked chain behind her neck.

As he turned her back to face him, he saw he'd judged the length perfectly. The teardrop stone landed exactly between her beaded nipples.

In truth, it was a gaudy specimen, the red rich and the size garish. He knew the naughty side of Thea would love it. Just as he knew she'd love the entwined strands of lustrous pearls that resided in the other box. The necklace he hoped to see her wear the next time he took her out.

And there would be a next time. Even had her reaction to discovering his speech debility not been as understanding as any man could wish for, Daniel knew he would've fought for her. Argued for her, long and loud. He would have exposed his every weakness for her sake because she made him strong.

A crack of thunder punctuated that thought, crashing right on top of the roof. For a change he didn't flinch, the welts on his arse didn't burn.

Because of her. The dark memories of his past had fled under the light she brought into his life.

Though the changes would no doubt take time, he was done with hiding. He had no plans to flagrantly flaunt his troubles, but neither did he want to let life—or love—pass him by.

"It's splendid," Thea said with an awed smile when she finally stopped looking down and met his gaze. "Thank you very much. Will I be thought unaccountably arrogant if I tell you to get in bed now?"

At her take-no-prisoner's tone, his brows flew upward but he was much too interested in what else she might tell him to do to demur. After all, how many lords were lucky enough to be ordered about by their lovely mistresses?

Stifling his grin, Daniel walked to his elaborate bed and provocatively situated himself in the middle of the huge mattress—never before had he so appreciated the excesses of the prior century.

"You do realize, do you not," she said from her position near his dresser, "that I'm going to have my wicked way with you and there's nothing you can do to stop me?"

And she thought he'd object?

She took a step forward. The ruby pendant

swayed. "Although…" she mused during the torturously slow step that followed, "I do expect something in return."

Entranced by the enticing swing of that damned nipple-red ruby, he made some sort of unintelligible grunt.

"What's that?" She just toyed with him, bringing her hand up to caress the stone. Then the vixen licked one finger and leisurely drew circles around each of her breasts. "You'll accede to anything I ask?"

By now she'd reached the foot of his bed.

By now his prick had pokered up stiff and straight.

By now he'd gladly forsake his birthright if only she'd climb over him and—

"I need a tuner posthaste," she said in a sensual voice that had nothing to do with her request. She brought one knee to the mattress and his heart into his loins. "My ears cannot take much more, you see."

Daniel had no idea what she was blathering about, not with her leaning seductively over his feet, trailing that deuced ruby over the tips of his toes, then across both ankles. He'd promise her the throne if only she'd come higher, skim that ruby over parts longer—and lonelier.

"The pianoforte is woefully misaligned." His brain refused to function when she reached up to unbind her hair, allowing it to drape past one shoulder and follow the path of the gem. "I don't think Buttons or Mr. and Mrs. Samuels can survive much longer, not with their hearing intact."

She laughed, dragged that stone up one shin and then the other. The strands of her hair followed, silken tendrils that wrapped around his will and tugged...tightened, rendering it nonexistent.

"I can tell I may need to remind you, when you're not..." She ringed each knee with ruby and hair, and the muscles in his thighs rippled, drawing her gaze to his groin. "Otherwise engaged."

His demure Thea had decamped, leaving a husky-voiced wanton in her stead. His eyes threatened to glaze over when she bent her head, pressed her lips to his skin, and marked a path for the ruby, sliding her mouth hotly over his inner thigh.

Like a man drunk on too much cheap jacky, his stomach clenched, heart hammered.

How quickly his mistress had gone from shy and trembling to bold and steady. From teasing his legs with the necklace to staring at his shaft. To approaching its hard length, the dangling chain forgotten as she climbed higher until poised above the patch of hair surrounding the root.

She licked her lips, a slow swipe of her tongue from one corner of her mouth to the other.

Her mouth—he'd always wondered what she could do with it.

What her plump lower lip would feel like curved around his anatomy.

You don't need to, his gentlemanly side wanted to shout.

Shut the blazes up! his baser side roared.

"I do believe..." she breathed over his erection

and damned if he didn't see it give a little jump. "I'm feeling freer than I ever have in my life."

She shifted to rest one bent arm on his thigh, dropping her chin upon her closed fist. Watching his face, she trailed the ends of her hair over his shaft, up and down, up and around.

When a deep gurgling noise came from the direction of his headboard, she smiled and swung her hair back. "Enough torture? Or mayhap not...?"

Playfully, she walked two fingers up the side of his abdomen. "I believe there exists something I've thought of doing," she kept staring right at him, "only since meeting you, mind, but I was hesitant to attempt it previously, unsure whether it was acceptable. But as someone told me recently..." She leaned forward and licked the crown of his penis with the very tip of her tongue. "If it feels right, 'tis no matter what the law says, wouldn't you concur?"

The law? Who the bloody hell had she been conversing with—about sex?

Who the bloody hell cared when she abandoned her relaxed stance and used her opened fist to clasp his cock and her walking fingers to clutch one side of his hips as she raised up and licked him again. Swirled her tongue around the crest of his erection before bringing it fully into her mouth. Before applying a bit of suction and offering up an appreciative *Mmmm*.

A sound which had him strangling on his excitement, forcing his buttocks back to the bed. Couldn't go scaring her off. Not when she gazed up at him and deliberately did it again. "*Mmmmmmm.*"

"God, Thea!" burst from him as his loins started shaking and one of his blunt nails pierced right through his bed sheets.

After a silent but fierce pull that curled his toes, she eased back. Running her thumb over the purpling head, she shot him a mischievous glance. "Appears I can assume you find that rather to your liking." Her fingers tightened around his shaft. "Then aren't you the fortunate one? For I've been practicing."

Practicing?

With a gleeful laugh, she took the crown back inside her mouth. Lips closed firmly around the corona, fingers snug on his staff, Thea answered his unspoken question in the most spectacular way.

"Hmmmmmmmmmmmmmmmmmmmm..."

And Daniel died and went to heaven.

HE WOKE EARLY the next morning, long before the light of dawn met the day, his body sated and heavy, his mind a jumble of so many erotic images it was hard to settle on just one.

Thea loving him with her mouth.

Thea stopping just when he moaned, a ragged sound that told her the end was near.

Thea gliding over him until she kissed his lips,

slanting her body until her feminine depths were within reach.

Thea, her hot and moist center enticing him inside, sliding so snugly around him that he'd never felt more at home.

Thea, whispering to him later as she rode above him and his hands tightened on the cheeks of her arse, dipping between a time or two, "We can do it there. If it would please you," and while his cock rejoiced and his heart cracked, she brought her chest to his, kissed beneath his ear and added, "Sometime soon, I'm thinking, but just not tonight."

Thea, the woman whose warm flesh hugged him skin to skin, no barriers—no preventative nor lies—in the way. It felt so natural, so right, being intimate with her without anything between them that Daniel never thought to question the lack. That told him something right there.

Told him he was bewitched. And not by one of Ellie's little spells, but by the sweet siren who uttered his name in a soft, silken voice. "Tonight, strong Daniel, I want to revel in loving you without any cumbersome uncertainties or self-doubts weighing me down. Time enough for another new amorous adventure in the future, hmm?"

Dazed, he nodded. Anything she wanted, anything. He wanted to be the one to provide it. Any—

"But I would like for you to touch me there, deeper. As you did at the opera. Ah...*mmm.*" When his finger greeted her anus, she gave a little cry and her loins surged against his just before the hot wash of her release bathed his shaft in wonder.

A huge, replete sigh heaved from him.

Never mind that the orgasm he recalled occurred hours ago, he still felt it in every pore of his being.

Thea, who'd made his dreams—ones he hadn't even been aware of—possible. Fact.

Thea, whom he loved and wanted for his own. It was time to tell her. Out loud.

Shaking off the drugging vestiges of sleep, Daniel blinked and rolled toward her: Thea, his love.

Thea. Who was gone.

5

A FAN – OR TWO – WHIPS UP A FLURRY

A short while earlier...

IT WAS STILL night when she woke. Dark beyond the edges of the curtains in Lord Tremayne's bedchamber.

Apprehension marked this particular occasion—because unlike the previous times she'd dozed and awoke, this time morning approached. She felt it with a foreboding in her bones.

Morning, which brought harsh, unavoidable realities with it.

Morning. Bah.

She'd growl if she could, for once it arrived, 'twould not do for her to be found in the master's bed. Nay, not when she was his *mistress*, a female relegated to a small and precise role in his life. One who had no right to be here.

Oh, but Daniel's breathing was steady, his warmth stretched out alongside hers divine, and Thea wanted nothing more than to linger.

A serene smile curved her lips. At least she'd finally spent the night in his arms. Only she'd never imagined it would be in *his* bed!

A sigh huffed gently from his lips, his breath brushing the top of her head and Thea's smile grew. In the next moment, his sleep-husked, nonsensical murmur met her ears as his arms tightened around her—almost as though, even in sleep, he sensed her intention to depart.

She willed her muscles to unclench, to sink deeper into his embrace and savor every second.

She'd slept in the same bed with Mr. Hurwell over two thousand two hundred nights—she'd calculated the depressing number at some point during the sixth year of their marriage. Yet after little more than a single full night, little less than a week total, she knew more genuine caring from the slumbering man holding her now than she ever had from her spouse.

But she had no time to wonder what dreams might be wandering through his mind, what recollections or regrets from the night. No time to ponder the number of minutes until daybreak. Nay, for before the household brimmed with activity, she intended to be back where she belonged.

.   .   .

THE STUNNING RUBY tucked beneath her bodice, stays laced as best she could manage in near silence—and by herself—Thea slipped out Lord Tremayne's bedroom door. Best she began thinking of him as she ought, save "Daniel" for the bedchamber. "Lord Tremayne", she reminded herself, was her protector —a man who paid for the privilege of using her body.

Paid generously and isn't the privilege all yours? some inner imp taunted.

Wall sconces lit the corridor and guided her toward the stairs. Fresh beeswax candles. What a luxury and how quickly she'd grown used to them herself. Such a departure from the candleless black nights she'd endured in recent months.

Tiptoeing down the massive staircase, she was battling guilt over the thought of rousing Buttons to take her home—she'd learned her lesson about roaming London alone—when the servant emerged from the shadows to meet her at the bottom of the stairs.

"He'll not like you sneaking off," Buttons told her with a frown.

"Sneaking!" she whispered back, ignoring the prickle of her conscience. "I'm doing nothing of the sort. I'm returning to my townhouse—where I belong."

Buttons crossed his arms over his chest, looking remarkably intimidating for all his youth. "He'd want you to stay."

"But it's nearly morning."

"Makes no matter."

Irritable because Buttons was only enticing her toward what she already wanted—and knew she shouldn't—Thea walked around him.

"Have it your way, Miss Thea." He sounded aggrieved but turned to follow.

"Don't you ever sleep?" she grumped at him, ashamed of herself when she heard the complaint emerge. "And where's my pelisse, do you know?"

"John will get it from Petie and bring it over later."

That stalled her determined exodus. "Who?"

"Mrs. Peterson, the housekeeper," he explained. "She hemmed the sleeves last night and I don't dare barge in asking for it at this hour."

Hemmed the sleeves? That marvelous man!

They were at the door. Buttons was big enough he could stop her if he chose.

"Please?" Thea said starkly, her gaze unwillingly drawn overhead to the ornate chandelier that graced the ceiling.

That fancy, expensive alliance of metal and glass only illustrated the difference in their stations. Her former ceiling, and the room she'd rented for months, had been water stained, smoke stained, and stained with the taint of the wretched hopelessness that had surrounded her on a daily basis.

She looked back at Buttons. "It's not my place to be here when the household arises. Take me home before everyone in Lord Tremayne's employ knows what I've done. Please?"

After a moment's consideration, he nodded once. "Before we go, I need to tell John that we're off. He had the first watch—that's when I slept. I spelled him a while ago, figurin' you'd try to sneak—er, *leave* early this morning."

He turned to go but immediately swung back. "And you're wrong, if I can say so without gettin' my lugs boxed. Ever'one here likes you jus' fine. Better than fine, I be thinkin'—because his lordship *really* likes you.

"There's fewer servants here than what you'd figure for a house this size, but we've been with him for years, those of us there are. Long before he got the title. An' we're all fiercely loyal to him. Not jus' because he pays us but because we choose to be. We care 'bout him."

At this point during his startling and informative revelation, Buttons gave a light shrug. "He cared about most of us first. Petie? She worked the tavern near the Tremayne Estate, serving and cleaning and motherin' all the local lads in Aylsham. Got turned out when she couldn't hear no more, an' after decades of hard work. When his lordship found out, he rode up to Norfolk and brought her here. I speak for ever'one when I say that you haven't got any censure to fear, not from us."

"No censure to fear..." Thea numbly repeated. It was easier to latch on to that particular phrase than the entire sentiment so eloquently and earnestly just expressed.

"Been workin' on elongating an' expanding my

vocabulary," Buttons said with a wink. "It impresses Sally Ann."

During the wee hours of the night, the quiet, still times between energetic lovings when Thea had slept cradled in his arms, Daniel had remained awake, thoughts brimming, plans forming, words being chosen. Decisions made.

He'd lived for years with his father's harsh disapproval. Some of his choices had been made to flaunt his defiance of the man's authority; more had been made to hide his difficulty.

Well, no longer. He was a man in love with his mistress, and he was man enough to do something about it. But before he tracked down his missing woman, and gave her a lecture on absconding with nary a word—with her person *and* his heart—he had first a relative and then a shopkeeper to see.

Dawn found him approaching Ellie and Wylde's townhouse from the mews, carefully picking his way through the rain-dampened ground. And not disappointed.

"Good," he greeted his sister who was hunkered down in the garden picking through a patch of something. "You're up."

Elizabeth flew to her feet with a startled cry, hand going to her neck. "Daniel! Since when do you rise with the chickens?"

Since he awoke without Thea.

He felt his lips curve at the picture his sister made, wearing old, mud-smeared clothes, intent on bringing life up from the cold and dormant soil. "Always reminds me of Mama, seeing you thus."

The fright left her gaze to be replaced with a flattered flush. "I love hearing you say so. I wish I could remember her."

Laden with her gardening tools, Ellie took a slow step forward and blinked at him in the gloom. "I cannot fathom what brought you here—and so early!"

"Can we t-talk?"

His odd request had her stripping off gloves and setting down the trowel. "Certainly. Come in. I doubt breakfast is ready but I'll have some tea brought— No? Why are you shaking your head?"

"I've ad-di-ditional errands," he told her, taking her arm to steer them toward a bench he'd noticed beneath a leafy tree. "D-don't want to run into Wylde. Just you this morning."

"You're here to take me to task for the opera, aren't you?"

"Nothing of the sort." Daniel had the sense they were being watched and craned his neck around.

"Trust me. He's never up at this hour. I didn't think you ever were either. Come, tell me what brings you here."

They settled on the stone bench, Daniel's gaze going to where he'd originally spotted his sister.

The smell of damp earth was strong. The growing cacophony of chirpy, whistling birds uplifting. As though they too wanted to sing in celebration of what he'd decided. Either that or they celebrated the cessation of rain.

"Daniel." Chastisement was in her tone. "That's the second time you've consulted your timepiece, and you here less than three minutes. I hardly ever see you do so. What has you acting so strangely?"

"I sent John round to Morrison's..." He mentioned the emporium he tended to frequent whenever needing to purchase a gift; a gift he typically let the proprietor choose and send with his name. But not this time. "To inquire whether he'd let me in early. I want to buy a fan for Thea. I noticed she d-didn't have one at the opera."

"A parting gift?" Elizabeth sounded aghast. Her fisted hands rose—as though she wanted to smack him!—before she brought them, shaking, back to her lap. "You should be ashamed! A fan—"

Daniel halted the tirade, placing his large gloved hand over both of hers. "Nn-*nay*. It rankles you should think me so cheap. A fan? As a *congé*? Pah. You're completely off the mark. I want her t-to have one I p-pick out, 'tis all."

"But a fan!" Her irritation over his choice of gift seemed completely over-the-top. Daniel let it slide when she changed the subject with, "You're unusually verbose today. Perhaps I should always schedule my visits at five minutes after sunrise?"

"When I'm usually snoring," he snorted on a smile. He squeezed her bare fingers. "Ellie. I would never d-do anything to harm you. But I find I must.

You are my one regret in this, how you will p-p-*pay* for my—"

She snatched her hand free and turned fully toward him. "You're frightening me. You aren't leaving England, are you? Are you sick? Injured? Where? What—"

Touched by her concern, he put one arm around her shoulders and pulled her close. "Nn-*nay*. Nothing of the sort. But I am hoping to be married—"

"Married!" Alarm made her pull back. Her eyes narrowed at him, steely glints in the slowly increasing light. "Now? But what about Thea? I mean Mrs. Hurwell?"

Not the reaction he'd expected. "What about her?"

"Ah...um. I have a confession to make—about your mistress. About Thea."

Why did Ellie look guilty?

"I went to see her yesterday and—"

"You..." He hadn't expected that. "What about?"

"My difficulties with Wylde, if you must know. I needed the advice of someone with more experience. Ah, in the bedroom."

She'd gone to Thea for sexual advice? Daniel was hard-pressed not to laugh.

For his unsuccessful attempt, he got summarily elbowed in the ribs. "Ow! Ellie. They're still sore."

"And I still owe you a jar of cream. But she was wonderfully helpful and, oh, Daniel, I like her very much. And now you're going to get married?" She sounded distraught. "End things with Thea?"

Never would he have expected such disapproval from this quarter. It hadn't escaped him either that Ellie expressed zero interest in his potential future wife; nay, all her concern was for his mistress.

Women!

Ellie sighed. "Thea's not at all what I thought a mistress would be."

Nay, she wasn't. "More like a wife."

"*What?* A wife!" He'd reduced his composed sister to shrieks.

At least they weren't critical shrieks. Nay, given her smile and the clapping and the jumping up and down, given the strangling hug she suffocated him with and the shout in his ear, he'd have to say they were shrieks of approval.

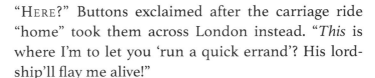

"Here?" Buttons exclaimed after the carriage ride "home" took them across London instead. "*This* is where I'm to let you 'run a quick errand'? His lordship'll flay me alive!"

In the act of getting down, Thea paused. She flashed a falsely confident smile. "He need never know. I only need one thing from my room—"

Buttons had already jumped to the ground and circled the carriage, as though to bar her from proceeding. At her explanation, he winced. "*Your* room, Miss Thea?"

She saw him look again, more warily this time, at their surroundings. The curve of the sun had just crested the horizon, giving him sufficient light to see the ugly street and uglier building she'd directed them to. Using Hatchards as a starting point, which she'd thought a stroke of brilliance, Thea had given her coachman Jem instructions.

"Aye. Until last week, this is where I lived." The confession was made without inflection.

People were beginning to stir, shutters banging open and the contents of slop jars and chamber pots being tossed into the streets.

Needing to get the distasteful task over with, she stood.

With a shudder, Buttons offered his arm to assist her down. "His lordship will have my head, but I can see sure-like you'll come back on your own later if I order us turned around now." After a severe frown at her, he glanced at the driver. "You see them two men over there, in that alley?" Buttons gestured with the back of his head. "Eyeing the mare, they are. Got your whip handy?"

"Aye, I do."

"Can't tell whether they want to eat her or steal her, but stay sharp." Then to Thea, as if issuing a dare, "Let's see jus' how fast you can be."

As she walked inside after several days' absence, heading down the narrow hallway to her room on the second floor, seeing—and smelling—the bleak accommodations, it struck Thea anew how far she'd sunk.

Was that why she'd insisted they return *this* morning, after she'd basked in the grandeur of her stolen, illicit night? Why, in spite of her valid desire to retrieve the brush her mother gave her, she felt compelled to remind herself—perhaps to show Buttons—how very much she *didn't* belong in Lord Tremayne's world?

But you don't belong here either, that intrusive inner voice insisted. *You, Thea Jane, were born to gentility. 'Twas shortsighted Hurwell and his selfish cousin who reduced you to these circumstances, condemned you to a future not of your choosing.*

Condemned? Time with Lord Tremayne felt anything but a punishment.

Ascending the rickety stairs, heading deeper into the bowels of the squalid place, especially after all the glitter and gleam she'd fallen into, made her recent past all that more embarrassing.

With every reluctant yet determined step, she was never more grateful for Buttons' solid presence at her heels.

Right before they reached the landing, a sharp double whistle rang out.

"That's Jem—on the carriage," Buttons told her in a low voice. He wavered in place.

"Go." She pointed down the way they'd just come. "We're almost there. I'll retrieve what I came for and meet you outside."

Not waiting for his agreement, she raced to her old room. The door was ajar. "Shouldn't be surprised," she muttered, pushing it wide, amazed to find any possessions remaining. In the grey light of dawn, she stepped to the old trunk that'd doubled as a dresser. Opening the hinged lid to search inside, she heard a tiny cry. Then another.

What was that?

The soft, persistent sounds came again from the corner and quickly bloomed into an all-out baby's wail.

So she had new neighbors on the other side of the wall? The strident cry of a hungry child, something she'd become benumbed to over the months of living in close proximity with so many people, unnerved her.

A baby.

Cherished brush in hand, Thea sat back on her heels and closed the trunk with a *thunk*.

A baby.

Oh Lord, the last two nights she'd forgotten to practice what Sarah had taught her. Nay, Thea realized with a gasp, she'd forgotten it *every* time. Had just assumed it was no longer necessary, not with how Lord Tremayne used the beribboned preventatives.

But at the opera—

And then last night in his bed—more than once!

Last night. The reminder of those precious hours softened the horror of her discovery. The prior eve, she'd been so very concerned for him, intent on showing him how much she cared naught about the stammer; how much she cared *for him.*

Well, blow me to Bedfordshire and back. A baby.

Loving him seemed so instinctive, so perfect, that she'd never thought to question the consequences.

Aye, her sensible side countered, *with a baby and out on your gullible backside—worse off than you were weeks ago if you aren't careful.*

Although that scenario paled in comparison to the idea of Daniel being gone from her life—his witty notes, his hearty laugh, the weight of his hard body coming into hers—

His arms holding her deep into the night.

If she was already enamored this much, after only a few days, what would happen in time, when she was thoroughly entranced by his spell?

Aren't you already?

"Not so bony anymore, are ya, eh?" A menacing voice hurled the accusation. "Almost didn't recognize that rounded arse on ya. That frilly dress."

Grimmett hauled a dazed Thea to her feet.

She'd been so lost in the fanciful imaginings of rocking Daniel's child, her mind far away from the sickening reality of her time here that it took several seconds to grasp who—and what—she now faced.

"Turned into a short-heeled wench after all. I always knew you were th' sort to fall on your back. Where's he keeping ya? Eh? Answer me, girly!" Grimmett twisted her arm when she remained silent.

Fear rushed in as though it had never left. The past week vanished and she was living on the edge of starvation. The sharp blade of terror.

"So the fancy toff's feedin' you more, I see. Or is it

more 'n one that's butterin' yer bun?" Every motion of his cracked lips revealed blackened teeth, blasted rotten breath into her face. "You workin' at Mother Mary's now? Makin' the beast with two backs with any man who gots a shiny coin? 'Sat why ya ain't been around?"

Her heart hammered so hard her chest hurt, limbs tensed so tight they squeaked. The days of meager hope looking for employment, evenings spent trying to block out the neighbors' yelled fights, and the long, rodent-filled nights of despair and hunger squeezed aside her newfound confidence.

Thea all but cowered.

"Don't deny you been whorin'—I kin smell it on ya."

"Nay." It was a whisper, a whimper.

He sniffed her neck, his black teeth snagging her skin as he rooted around like a mole scavaging grubs. "Got the scent of a well-prigged woman..."

She squirmed for freedom.

This couldn't be happening.

It was over! This horrid part of her life. The despicable things she'd eaten, the dirty clothes worn day after day. The tussles with Grimmett. Always watching over her shoulder for him—and others of his ilk. The terror. The *bugs*. Over, by damn!

"Think yer too good for ol' Grimmett, do ya? Always did act like you was above ever'body." He tightened his hold on her wrist and twisted harder. Inches away, his fetid breath assaulted her nose. "I see them fancy, peer-bought duds yer wearing. Can spread your legs for a toff's penny but not Grimmett's?"

She watched in a self-inflicted stupor as his tongue circled narrow lips. His gaze flicked to her chest, eyes gleaming when they caught sight of the chain nestled beneath the bodice.

No! The word got locked in her throat.

God, no!

Fight, Thea!

He reached for it. "What ya hiding here?" He fingered the chain, then gave a yank. When it didn't budge, he slammed her back into the wall and covered one breast. His fingers squeezed cruelly. "Not looking so high and fine, are ya? Just a sniveling street whore is all you are, all ya ever were."

Bile rose in her throat, choked off her air.

He released her wrist and clamped his dirty fingers on her bodice. The material ripped at his downward heave, making way for his insistent fingers to clutch at her bared breast, for his other hand to snatch at the ruby while he pinched and clawed at her nipple.

But his words had unlocked the paralysis imprisoning her limbs. Sniveling street whore, accused Grimmett.

I do have it in my head that he's a snivler, proposed Lord Tremayne in one of his first letters. *Your dear Mr. Freshley...*

Lord Tremayne. *Daniel.*

Her *dear* protector!

In the eyes of God and man, she might be no

better than a street whore. And the elevated new status she enjoyed just might come crashing down as soon as Lord Tremayne tired of her, but by all that was good and fun, joyful and right, by God, she wouldn't let anyone take away a single day of her happiness.

Especially not Grimmett.

Unfrozen, Thea kicked and screamed. The brush she'd forgotten she held cracked across his skull.

Her sudden ferocity startled Grimmett. His hold loosened a fraction. Just enough for her to break free. "No, you don't!" she yelled. "You won't touch me ever again!"

She floundered with the drooping bodice, pressing it high across her chest, and wielded the brush again. "Never!" She whacked him again. "You rotten—" Again. "Rotten mouse turd!" *Snap!* The wooden handle split. But her thrashing didn't pause. "You maggoty—"

"Miss Thea!" Buttons charged through the doorway, taking the situation in at a glance. He jerked Grimmett around and planted him a facer.

Incensed at the unexpected interruption, the landlord only spit and came forward for more. While Buttons struggled with the enraged man's flailing arms, Thea dropped the hairbrush, sparing not a thought to its newly broken state, and grabbed up the heaviest thing at hand—an old boot of Mr. Hurwell's. A mateless boot she'd used more than once to scoop up unwanted, multi-legged or whiskered visitors. Grasping it at the top, waiting for the precise moment between the grappling men, she swung. The heavy heel landed solidly against Grimmett's hard head. Finally stunned, he sank against the wall.

She opened her mouth to yell at him some more but Buttons launched himself between them. Assured she was unharmed, he took off his jacket and draped it around her shoulders, ushering her to the carriage after issuing a threat to the older man.

Thea had thought *she'd* learned some ribald slang during her stint in the rough area. Buttons' menacing warning, delivered in colorful and crude terms, actually had her ears stinging more than her abused breast.

Nothing, however, burned more than her pride.

Upon returning home after the encounter with Grimmett, three unexpected gifts awaited Thea.

One, a lacy ecru fan from Lady Wylde, tied to a note expressing her appreciation for Thea's company and the education she'd helped impart.

The note was read hurriedly—under the guise of pretending that accepting presents from titled ladies for Instruction in Mistressing Arts was nothing out of the ordinary. This farce was enacted given how *Lord Tremayne* looked on.

Aye, Lord Tremayne. Who Thea considered the second—and best—gift of the three.

Whose actual presence, given all that'd gone on

since she'd left his abode a scant time earlier was nearly sufficient to reduce her to a watering pot of epic proportions.

Thankfully, that cowardly urge was countered by the lifting of her spirits the moment she saw him waiting in her entry. Once she processed that he'd come after her—and so soon.

He smiled a bit sheepishly when Thea hurried in, still covered in Buttons' coat.

Her instinctive rush toward him was checked with his greeting words.

"Ap-p-pears I'm not your only admirer," he said ruefully, quickly stashing something behind his back. "I'll let you open that one first, see who it's from."

Though he glanced with interest at the fan, shown to its frilly perfection on the usually empty silver tray, his expression held no accusation, only indulgent curiosity.

Crossing into the sanctuary of her home, taking in everything at a glance and resolved to behave normally, Thea just barely avoided launching herself into his arms.

She sensed Buttons' frowning disapproval at her back. Could she help it if she was loath to explain, to relive the past hour? Better to forget it ever happened. So after quickly refolding the note from Lady Wylde, she used a magnified fascination with the pretty fan as an excuse to avoid looking at Daniel, concerned her expression would certainly convey The Unpleasant Incident.

The incident *already forgotten*.

"A fan! How lovely." Her voice only shook a lot. "I —I've—" She swallowed and tried again. "I've b-been wanting one. It's so nice of—of—" She couldn't very well tell Lord Tremayne that *his sister* had paid her a call. Certainly couldn't meet his eyes when she felt him come up behind her and saw that he, impossibly, held out a fan as well.

Easier to latch on to the incongruous sight of the striking specimen captured gently in his strong, masculine fingers. Easier to keep her neck bent, her head down, her gaze far away from the mirror glaring at her.

Unlike the delicate, lacy one his sister had chosen, the heavier fan he presented would whip up a gale. The screen was thick enough, when he fanned it out to reveal an intricately painted peacock upon the black silk, that she couldn't see the light through it.

"I was looking for something softer, more frilly in d-design, but this one caught my eye and I knew it was p-perf— Thea?"

"It is perfect. L-lovely, in fact." Her face felt uncomfortably warm as she reached to stroke the decisive pleats, to run the pad of one finger over the colorful bird at home within its folds.

Mayhap she could hide behind it? Bring it up in front of her face and sneak upstairs with no one the wiser. "From none to two in one—one m-m-morning—"

It was difficult to speak through the lump

swelling her throat. The unshed tears growing dense and hot now that she no longer put on a brave front for Buttons. Now that she was home. Now that *he* was here.

She gave a frantic laugh. "I now have two fans." When only minutes ago she'd been fanless. And accosted. Oh Lord! Another helpless giggle escaped. "T-two *fans!*"

"Thea. Sweetheart." Lord Tremayne stepped closer and curved both hands firmly around her upper arms, pulled her toward him. The line of the folded fan dug into one and she focused on the sensation. "Nnn-*nay!*" he directed over her shoulder, speaking to Buttons, she assumed, "d-don't frown at me again, mouth at me to wait. Her entire body is trembling and— What's this she's wearing...your coat?" And *there* was the accusation she'd expected when he'd noticed the gift from another. "Swift John? T-talk, man!"

"Aye, my lord, 'tis mine." She heard him shuffle in place. "Miss Thea, will you be telling him? Or do I?"

"One of you b-better." The rasp vibrated through her.

She shook her head so hard the coat slid from one shoulder. Nay! She didn't want to tarnish what they had now with her unpleasant past—

"Thea!" Lord Tremayne hissed, his hand following the path of the fallen coat. "Your neck— The chain! It's d-dug into your skin. D-dammit! You're bleeding." Warm fingers caressed across her nape to ease the metal free. Only then did she become aware of the burning where the chain must've sliced into her when Grimmett tried to rip it free.

Shuddering from the reminder, she wiggled from Daniel's gentle touch. "'Tis nothing. Let's forget—"

"Thea." With heavy hands to her shoulders, he shook her once.

She couldn't hide her wince. Neither could she avoid Lord Tremayne's gaze.

Lord Tremayne. Daniel. Lord Tremayne.

She didn't know what to call him anymore. How to think of him. Her past, her present, *their* present, spun her around till she was in knots.

"Daniel." Unbidden, his name, the *right* name, slipped from her lips at the worried concern in his gaze.

"I'm here, sweetheart. Now what..." As his fingers dipped beneath the coat to reveal the shattered state of her dress, his face did an incredulous turn from troubled to livid. He swore, coloring the air with curses that put Buttons' to shame. But when he fingered the torn bodice, when he glided one fingertip over the budding bruises from Grimmett's savagery, his touch was featherlight. "Talk to me, Thea. Who d-did this?"

At the solemn query she dove into his arms, needing to feel them around her, needing his strength, his scent, to obliterate the hateful, hurtful morning. "Please," she implored, her words muffled by his warm body, her eyes shut, frantic heartbeat only now calming. Now that she was with him. "I just want to forget."

She wrapped her arms around his waist and pressed her stinging breast hard against his chest.

Though he held her tight, brushing comforting palms down her back, his posture was steel, breathing choppy. "Swift John? Start t-talking."

"We went to her room, my lord. The one in Seven Di—"

"Seven Dials!" The syllables scratched like blades across boulders. "D-devil take you, you t-t-took her there? *Her?*"

"Don't." Thea wedged her arms against his chest to snare his gaze. "Don't blame him. I insisted. I—"

"Have t-totally ruined my surprise," he said in a doleful tone. He leaned down to kiss her forehead. "But it'll keep. Where else d-d-d—" His eyes squeezed shut, then flashed open, went to her torn bodice and a feral gleam lit their depths. "Hurt you elsewhere?"

"He didn't. Buttons intervened and it's over. Let's just forget this—"

"Go upstairs." He released his hold, his gaze on her torn skin. "T-take care of—"

"Go?" She clutched his arms. "Come with me."

His jaw firmed to granite. "Nn-*nay*." Hands to her waist, he pushed her from him. "Need to see this taken care—"

"This? Grimmett, you mean? Buttons already hit him!" She tried to lace their fingers, to tug him upstairs, but he avoided the maneuver. "Please? 'Tis over and done."

"Miss Thea clobbered him too," Buttons put in. "Don't think he'll trouble her again."

"Of course he won't!" she cried, just wanting it all erased. "I've no reason to go back. Let's just—"

"D-did you flatten him?" Daniel asked Buttons, ignoring her completely.

"Aye. But the bastard's still breathing."

"You can't mean to kill him," she said when some manner of unspoken, masculine accord passed between the men and they headed for the door. "He won't bother me again. I won't go back, I promise! *I've no reason to!*" If the shrill way she screeched after them was any indication, the morning had finally caught up with her.

Daniel returned. He smoothed one hand down the side of her head, skimmed his thumb over her cheek until he cupped her jaw. "Thea. Why d-did you go?"

"My brush," she replied miserably. "My hairbrush. 'Twas a gift from my mother. But his rotten skull cracked the wood, so it's pointless. Pointless for you to return."

Daniel's thumb dragged over her bottom lip. "D-don't you see? If not you, then another helpless woman—"

"I am not helpless! I walloped him good!"

"With a boot, no less," Buttons supplied. Rather unhelpfully, Thea couldn't help but think now that exhaustion claimed her and she simply wanted to wash off grimy Grimmett's abhorrent touch and sleep for a week.

Daniel meshed their lips for one heart-stopping moment. He spoke to her without words, expressing his frustration, his fears, and his desperate desire to see her unharmed. Without a sound uttered between them, she knew he wouldn't let it go.

When he gentled the pressure and raised his head, she reached for his hand, liberating the fan he still held. She waved it near his temple. "All right. Since I doubt you bought this for me to knock some sense into you, I'll accede. With reservations, mind." She carried his hand to her lips and kissed his fight-hardened knuckles. "No one else should be intimidated by him, you're right on that. But I cannot condone murder." She gave him an arch look.

"How about I rip off his b-ballocks and feed the rats?"

"Well, if you have the peace of mind to jest about it, then I suppose I can allow you to go." Obviously humor and sense had overridden fury and he no longer intended to kill the man. Or so she reasoned. On tiptoe, she kissed his cheek. "I await your return."

Holding up her bodice, she slipped over to Buttons and shrugged off his coat. "Thank you," she told him quietly, transferring it to his hands. "See he comes to no harm."

As the men took their leave, their parting exchange left her gasping.

"No harm?" Buttons laughed. "I'm to protect that pustule from you?"

"Nay. Thea meant pr-protect me, I b-believe," Daniel rejoined, a smile in his voice. "Foolish woman, she thought I was *joking*?"

"So we *are* servin' the sod's stones to the rats? Capital!"

6

PROTECTING HIS OWN BRINGS
THINGS UP TO SCRATCH

JUST OUT OF earshot of the door, Daniel turned to Swift John and grinned. "Think she heard?"

"Clear enough not to go wanderin' in places she oughtn't."

"Good." Waving off the driver, Daniel took the reins. "We have a stop to make. We'll b-b-*be* picking up another."

"Are ye certain, milord?" Jem asked from the ground. "Was a rough place, mighty interested in Callisto here. Don't trouble me none to go back." He patted the whip slung round his neck, then lifted his coat to show he'd armed himself further since their return.

"On second thought, climb on. Think I'll spell Calli, swing b-by and harness Jupit-ter instead."

"Sounds a right idea." Swift John jumped on the

seat beside him when Daniel motioned for the footman to join him, the coachman pulling himself up on the back.

"Lord Tremayne," Swift John began formally once they were off. "I surely regret this morn. Know you'd never forgive me if something had happened to—"

"You're d-damn right I wouldn't have!" Daniel exploded. Then just as quickly calmed himself. No sense getting angry at the wrong person when the right person waited at the end of a carriage ride. "She was d-determined to go. Remember that d-day she got lost? Before I sent you to her?"

"John's complained more than once he's missing out on all the fun. Today was anything but. Scared me, it did, seeing that filthy scourge attack her." He swallowed audibly. "Shouldn't have happened. Not on my watch. Would understand if—if...you sacked my soddin' arse."

"Don't talk nonsense," Daniel barked. They rolled along in silence, his tense grip on the reins conveying his agitation to the mare who picked up speed. "I'm thankful you were with her, Swi..." He trailed off, deciding to try something new. "Glad you were there, B-Buttons."

After mangling the man's preferred name, Daniel glanced over. His footman beamed, noting the change.

Then a haunted look came into his valued servant's eyes. Buttons leaned in, pitched his voice low. "Yer lordship. Godalmighty! You shoulda seen it. 'Twas a tiny hovel in the worst part o' the stews. She was blame near sleeping on rags!"

It took real effort to keep his expression bland, to not let on how much that news affected him.

"Since I d-don't want any of us d-dancing on air with a knot around our n-n-necks, and I'm liable to kill him in truth if I get in more than one rammer—hell, one might d-do it, the way I'm feeling—we're stopping to p-pick up Tom Everson." The long-winded explanation surprised Daniel. He never explained. He never talked, not when he could avoid it.

But still, the words kept gushing forth, the memory of the dried blood on Thea's neck, the torn dress, the way she burrowed into his chest when she finally admitted what happened... It all made him want to rip limbs from the lecher, and damned if talking didn't ease the rage. "He's ab-b-out your age, a fighting enthusiast without much experience. B-but with loads of heart."

"Happy to have another set of fives," Button said, rubbing his together. "'Specially if yours are sitting out."

Daniel's hands flexed upon the reins. "I'm d-det-t-*termined* to teach this Grimmett b-bastard a lesson, though. For Thea and anyone else he's harmed. And...Buttons"—Daniel shot him a grim glance as he pulled around the back of his townhouse, heading to the mews for a fresh horse and a less attractive carriage—"'t-tis your and Tom's job t-to make sure I conduct myself in a manner that won't have Thea tearing off *my* b-ballocks for a rat snack."

THEY PICKED up more than Jupiter, though, when Daniel's regular driver Roskins learned of their mission.

"I'm from there, milord. Still know my way around. Might just come in handy."

"Jump on."

As he'd hoped, Tom made an eager addition and, once the lanky redhead came aboard, the five of them were soon abandoning the parts of the city they frequented in reluctant favor of the slums.

Where the streets were narrow, the houses crumbling, and the smells atrocious.

"That's it."

"Here 'tis, milord."

Jem and Buttons spotted their destination at the same moment.

Leaving the two coachmen with the carriage and Buttons stationed at the door to prevent an escape should Grimmett think to attempt one, Daniel and Tom went in search of the louse-riddled landlord.

The whiny, grease-faced Grimmett proved easy to find, for he'd made no friends in the area and more than one tenant was eager to give up his location—even before Daniel offered a coin.

All too soon, the wretch sagged to the floor. And

with very little effort extended upon either of their parts.

Tom roared forward for another swing, ready to defend the honor of the lovely woman he'd met the night he came looking for Daniel. But he was too late. With a feeble cry, the sorry-arse excuse for a man scrambled drunkenly out the door.

Buttons popped his head in. "Want me to run him down? It'd be a right pleasure."

Daniel considered a moment before answering with a slight shake of his head. On the drive over, he and Roskins had devised a plan whereby his coachman's cousin, who still lived in the area, would keep an eye on the beetle-headed recreant. Satisfyingly, Grimmett was already in half mourning when they'd found him, thanks to the chop Buttons had landed earlier. Or possibly it was Thea's boot swinging that had blackened the bastard's eye (his footman had regaled them with details of the morning's encounter on the way).

"Just m-m-*make* sure he stays gone while we're here."

"Aye, your lordship." As Buttons crossed back into the hall, a ragged cat streaked inside.

Hissing at Daniel and Tom, it raced to a corner and ducked beneath a ratty-looking chest of drawers.

"C-c-c-c-can't believe anyone wwwwould want to-to-to live here that bad." Tom followed the flash of dirty grey. "Hey, b-b-boy, don't you want-t-t to-to come on out?"

Daniel looked around. There wasn't anything

worth salvaging. The brush Thea had come for had cracked, splintered wood snagging on his coat pocket when he tucked the halves inside.

The walls might have been relatively clean, a swipe of his gloved finger across one told him, but no amount of washing could disguise the pallor that permeated the room. The squalidness that surrounded it just steps away. He couldn't believe Thea had been relegated to such dingy and depressing environs. How remarkable that she'd remained so bright and lively—

"He's b-b-bleeding." Tom's voice was muffled. "Come on, k-k-k-itty— Ow!" At the surprised cry, Daniel left off his frowning inspection and walked the mere two paces to the corner.

"Got me, he d-d-d-did." Tiny slashes of red welled from three close-set cuts on the back of Tom's hand. "Sharp claws, that's f-f-f-for sure!"

Another Mr. Freshley?

Daniel knelt to face the growling feline. A smear of dried blood matted several whiskers. The cat hissed and he noticed more blood, redder and wetter, on his chin.

If the blame animal wanted to guard this hovel, he was welcome to it. Daniel tensed his thighs to stand but the plaintive mew the cat gave made him pause. What? Ol' grumpy-puss here wanted attention now? "'Tis all right, Mr. Freshley," Daniel soothed, shifting a fraction closer and keeping his arms tucked safely out of clawing reach. "Let's have a look at you. Find out where that bl-blood—"

"Lookit-it here, D-Dan!" Tom's excited whisper caught his attention.

Seeing where the boy gazed, Daniel peered under the rickety chest.

Only to be confronted with undeniable proof of his mistake.

He turned back to the cat, crossed his arms over his chest. "So, *Mrs.* Freshley, how would you and your rat's nest of kittens like a nice home?"

Moments later, after acknowledging the kittens and their grumpy mama were the only things of value in the room (and theirs dubious), Daniel walked into the hallway and shouted for Buttons.

After he made his request, his footman looked at Daniel as though he'd lost his marbles and the bag they came in. "You want me to *what*?" his servant exclaimed. "Find a padded box for six kittens?"

"Aye, and her too." He pointed to Mrs. Freshley, who'd followed him into the hallway once she realized he didn't intend to harm her brood. "Only b-better make hers a *locked* b-box.

"And get a blanket to wrap her in. Oh, and grab the thickest gloves you can," Daniel added, idly wondering why it was easier to contemplate facing a two-hundred-and-fifty-pound opponent in the ring than a scrawny, fur-covered feline. Something to do with those sharply pointed front teeth, perhaps? "I'd rather not ruin my nice p-pair."

"I'll see what Roskins an' Jem have. Between us, we'll get the little ones and their mama corralled."

The female in question had been rather industrious during their exchange.

When Buttons went off to find suitable cat-catching equipment, Daniel hunkered down to address the newest member of his household. "You'll have one job, Mrs. Freshley—n-nay, make that t-two. Feed those youngsters and b-be *nice* to your new mistress. That's how you'll earn your keep."

The cat just blinked at him, licking her lips and daring Daniel to say a word about the fresh blood on her paw or the mouse tail—suspiciously lacking a mouse body—just behind her.

AFTER DROPPING off an exhilarated Tom and his well-fed servants at their respective lodgings (he'd treated everyone to a thumping good beef steak at a local alehouse Roskins recommended)...

After depositing one very vocal mama cat back with her kittens—"They'll be right fine under my watchful eye, Lord Tremayne," his housekeeper Mrs. Peterson told him quietly and precisely, as she always spoke. "I'll see she has some cream and part of tonight's ham." (Tonight's ham—Daniel's supper? Wondrous. Now *he* was reduced to table scraps?)...

After he washed the stench of the stews off his person and talked (ha!) Crowley out of shaving his jaw (time was precious and hadn't Thea told him she'd come to like his whiskers?)...

After. After. *After.*

Seemed it took an age to arrive at Thea's town-house, Cyclops in tow. A dreamily dribbling Cy whose constant barking (and resultant drooling) professed his pleasure at the unexpected outing.

Daniel couldn't wait to converse with Thea. Aye, *converse.* To jabber, to jaw. Hell, he wanted to rhapsodize with her. Share his past, convince her to share his future.

But as she'd done from the moment they met, she stumped him once again. Because instead of eagerly awaiting his return, she was upstairs asleep. And softly *snoring*, he realized after he spoke with Mrs. Samuels and showed himself up.

"Said she wanted to know the second ye arrived," the housekeeper had told him downstairs. "Tried to rouse her, I did, when Sam spotted your horse, but the wee thing is done in. Fell into bed the moment we got her washed up."

Here, she'd paused for breath, her gaze drifting to Cy and the puddle he'd left on her entry floor. Least it wasn't piss—something Daniel would've quipped out loud if Thea, and not the housekeeper, stood before him.

"Yer dog, my lord," Mrs. Samuels said gingerly, bravely venturing a hand to pat Cy's head (and of course prompting that long pink tongue to loll and more drool to fall), "shall I take him to the kitchen? Find a bone..."

Cy whined and leaned into Daniel's leg.

"Ap-pears he wants to see his new mistress. My new marchioness," Daniel said with a straight face, keeping his gaze on Mrs. Samuels.

The woman indulged in a bit of drooling of her own.

To hide his smile, he bent to blot Cy's puddle with his ever-present handkerchief.

"Oh, my lord!" exclaimed Mrs. Samuels once she recovered and saw his actions. "Ye shouldn't be doing that!"

"'T-tis only spit. I can wipe it up as well as anyone." Rising, he pointed up the stairs with his walking stick. "Go." Cy bounded up at the invitation.

"Miss *Thea*?" the housekeeper all but stammered. "Yer new marchioness?"

"If she'll have me." Daniel gave a wink, then sauntered after his dog, tossing over his shoulder, "Please see that we aren't d-dist-t-turbed."

For once, the wretched blunder didn't make him cringe. Far too many more important things lay on his tongue.

"Aye, my lord!"

WATCHING Thea sleep proved an exercise in torture.

It was torture seeing her hair down, long and lustrous, tangled upon the pillow cushioning her head and restraining himself from trying to unknot the strands. Torture seeing that pretty pink mouth part when she groggily rolled over, stopped snoring (which made him smile) and made a tiny *hmmm* in her throat (which made him hard).

Torture watching her fingers seek the black handle of the fan he'd given her, just peeking out from beneath her pillow, until she found it and made another drowsy *hmmm* before drifting back under.

Torture keeping Cy from drowning in his own doggie-style euphoria as his tail thumped and he grinned at the lady occupying the big bed—alone.

Finally, after more than one unsuccessful attempt to gently rouse her, too impatient to wait any longer, Daniel released his hold on Cy's collar and pointed.

After a running start, the lumbering dog cannoned onto the bed.

The echo of his landing likely shook the walls downstairs.

It certainly shook Thea awake.

DRIPPY LICKS MET HER CHEEK, an excited bark, her ear.

But it was the husked, "Cy, don't d-drown her," that lured Thea from the depths of slumber.

She wiped at the cool wetness coating her ear and encountered a moist muzzle. "Cyclops?" Heavy eyelids shuttered open to the music of exuberant pants. Only to find the dainty chair painted with trailing roses across her chamber occupied by one very *un*-dainty masculine specimen.

"Lord Tremayne?" Thea jerked upright. Daniel was here?

The opposite of her suddenly tense posture, he lounged—as much as a powerful presence could upon such feminine furniture. By candlelight, she drank him in. His tailcoat was discarded, hanging haphazardly from the arm of the chair. In shirt, simple neckcloth and burgundy waistcoat, thick hair decidedly mussed, shadow of whiskers on his jaw temptingly dark, he devastated her senses.

Kiss *now*. Hold *now*. *Love forever*, was all Thea could think. Notions she had no right to.

You're here for his convenience. His. She reminded herself of one of Susan's less bawdy teachings.

Oh, but he was in her room, looking for all the world as though he had no intention of ever leaving. That made her smile. "I must be dreaming."

She had to be, surely, if she was starting to convince herself *he* belonged here. With her.

His paid whore. That unpalatable reminder made her wince. Self-conscious now, she brought a hand to her cheek. Rubbing back the strands of hair that'd stuck to the side of her face, she felt sleep creases in her skin. "I must look a fright."

"Nay, not now nor the last t-t-two t-times you awoke. Here." He rose and brought her a glass. "And it's D-Daniel, lest you've forgotten."

"Thank you." *Last two times?* Groggily trying to remember, Thea sipped.

"There's a tray t-too, when you're hungry."

The expectant glint sparking from his eyes put the glow of the hearth to shame. Her brow pinched as hazy scenes surfaced. "It's all murky. But I seem to recall you talking, telling me of your grandfather and...and..."

Fresh new memories swirled in her rapidly clearing mind, the fog of sleep blurring some, but she pieced together enough to summon the truth.

He'd told her how, a scant year after his beloved twin fell to his death, both his mother and older brother succumbed to a fever that decimated the townsfolk near their estate. How a young Daniel and even younger Ellie had been left to the "miserable mercy" of a grieving and inconsolable father.

A sire who hired a tutor and forbade Daniel the private school education every other boy of his rank experienced as his due. A sire who blamed a neighboring boy, one who grew to become his brother-in-law Lord Wylde, because he'd brought the fever from the village to the outlying estates.

A sire who punished every misspoken word.

A child who learned 'twas better to keep silent than risk inciting his father's wrath. Wrath that was sometimes visited on his innocent sister as well.

Just when Thea felt the bitter salt of welling tears, she recalled his stories of a loving and aged grandfather, father to his deceased mother, a man confined to a wheeled chair, eventually to a bed. A relative who'd expressed more than once his desire to raise Elizabeth and Daniel but who recognized his own limitations. So he'd done what he could, Daniel had told her, setting aside funds for both of them, encouraging whatever they'd shown an interest in. Inviting them for visits until their father discovered how ill the old man had become and put a stop to it.

A short time later, their treasured grandfather was gone too.

Daniel had shared how fighting—boxing—proved his salvation. The one place he could be surrounded by his peers and feel a part of the camaraderie. When he used his fists, he didn't have to say a word. He'd been liked, respected even, for his prowess. And with every punisher he'd received, he'd considered it deserved—paying the price for daring David to climb up after him...

He'd glossed over his childhood but she'd gleaned enough in the flat telling of what he revealed, in the stark look he couldn't hide, to discern what had been a disheartening existence. She'd learned of a young man escaping his father's restrictive rule the moment he was big enough to fight back, of how he'd set up his own home in London, his only regret the sister he couldn't lure to join him. A sister who by now was their father's caretaker as much as his prisoner.

As though commiserating with his master, Cyclops plopped his woebegone-expressive muzzle on her shoulder. Thea paused her racing thoughts to give a big scratch on his damp chin.

Words. There'd been so many. Hordes of them.

Syllables—too many to count. The blessed, cherished sound of Lord Trem—of *Daniel's* voice, telling her so much of what she'd longed to hear.

"I remember now." She placed the empty glass on the night table and reached for his hand. "Tell me I didn't imagine it all."

"'T-tis all true." He nudged Cyclops aside and sat on the edge of her bed. "You fell asleep during the telling of it."

"I would never!" Drat her to Dartmoor, he finally opens up and she goes off to nod?

"You d-*did*."

Avoiding what looked suspiciously like a smirk to her, Thea reached behind her to plump the pillows. "Well. I am wide awake now and quite...um, delighted to have you in my room."

"D-delighted, eh?" The confident wretch laughed at her.

His duty done, Cyclops settled at the foot of the bed, tail occasionally giving a good *thump*.

"Aye! *Delighted*," Thea fairly snarled, plucking the fan from where the handle persisted in poking her posterior. She moved the latch and spread the spokes. Flicking her wrist, she attempted a flirty move. It came off agitated.

A blunt fingertip drew the fan away from her face. "Thea?"

Mayhap one in revealing nightwear was meant to entice, not avoid.

And that was another thing—she *finally* dons the

night rail he gave her on the very night he wants only to *talk*?

"Oh, very well." She snapped it shut and met his gaze. "If you must know, I'm humiliated. How could I drift off when *you* finally turn up verbose? It's very poorly done of me!"

He pried the fan from her tense grip and brought her hand to his mouth where he bestowed several gentle kisses upon her knuckles. Only once the tension drained from her arm did he stop. "No more of that now. I d-did not mind. So you shall not either."

"But I—"

He bent his head and slipped her index finger into his mouth. And *suckled* it.

She felt the pull all the way down to her toes. His tongue swirled around the digit as the heat in his eyes became unbearable.

"All right!" Thea conceded with ill grace as her arm melted to cinders. "I'm allowed to fall asleep on you without *ever* feeling remorse. Now do please leave off before I turn to ash!"

Wearing a self-satisfied smile, he pulled her finger free, then carefully, thoroughly, dried it on his tight-fitting pantaloons.

"Wicked, are you," she breathed as she felt the hard muscles of his thigh flexing beneath her finger. "And even *more* wicked," she accused after he finished his task and pressed her fingers to his groin before relocating her hand to the mattress—inches away from his leg.

He only smiled, making no mention of his aroused state. Mayhap talking wasn't *all* he intended.

"Have you anything to ask me, b-b-before I proceed?"

"Proceed?"

"With what I came to tell you."

That sounded ominous. It also put to bed thoughts of things other than talking. "There's *more*?"

"Quite."

"Ummm," Thea stalled. The tingling from her arm had affected her tongue. "How long have you been in my room? Watching me sleep? Or should I say waiting for me to wake?"

He grinned, a boyish, carefree curve of lips that brought the laughter into his eyes, that dimple to his cheek. "Counted eleven whistles from that illustrious cuckoo clock d-down the hall."

She smiled back. "You've restored my faith in clocks."

"Me?"

"You and that particular design. No mean feat, I assure you. I'd quite come to hate the wretched things. But now I only find them *inspiring*."

"As well I know." Daniel inclined his head, what else he wanted—*needed*—to say burning a hole in his gut. "Anything else?"

If so, she'd better ask now because once he started with the rest, he doubted he could stop. His throat was as sore as a goose's golden-egg-laying arse. Knew he'd pay for it tomorrow, but he wouldn't be able to stop until the rest was out.

"Thea?" She looked so much more alert now, still sleep-flushed and inviting but more aware than she'd been the last time they'd spoken.

He shouldn't have been surprised, really. She'd been viciously attacked that morning and wide awake most of last night, vigorously making love. With her doing creative things and taking command of all the conversation; with him simply lying back and loving every second. By all accounts, he should be dead on his feet too, ready to climb under those covers with her and doze until daybreak but he was too worked up to relax.

"Is Grimmett still breathing?" Even as she asked, he saw her rub the finger he'd just bathed.

"Was the last time I saw him." *Crawling away like the coward he is.* "More's the pity."

In the hours he'd been there, rehearsing what was to come, Daniel reasoned against telling her the likely fate of her royally named rodents. That, thanks to Mrs. Freshley's appetite, in all probability he'd brought them over to his household as well. Parts of them, at least.

"After you left, I considered what you said." She left off staring at her finger to fix a worried gaze on him. "How can we be sure he won't assault others?"

"He won't."

"But you don't *know* that," Thea persisted.

"Oh, but I d-d-do." And because she kept looking

at him, so trustingly yet quizzically, he explained what he'd intended to keep to himself. "Roskins' cousin is going to keep an eye on Grimmett."

"Why would he do that?" She sounded baffled.

"B-be-be*cause* he's a good man."

"And...?"

Daniel heaved a big sigh. Mouse tails aside, mayhap 'twas best not to keep any more secrets from Thea. "I offered to fund ap-p-prenticeships for his three boys and t-two girls. He works the docks—or did until his arm got crushed."

She grasped the ramifications immediately. "And now he's having trouble providing for his family?"

Daniel nodded. "B-but he's an intimidating hulk who can still use the left one to p-pound away if Grimmett crosses the line."

The admiration in her expressive eyes nearly brought Daniel to the blush. By the devil!

"Your brush," he blurted without any finesse, "was splintered ab-b-bominably."

Admiration faltered to dismay. "I know." She curved her arm through his and leaned into him until she rested along his side, head on his shoulder. "But it was sacrificed for a good cause. Mama would be pleased it cracked smashing such a sap-filled, rotten skull."

Despite the smile her words wrought, Daniel felt her loss. He pressed a soothing kiss to the top of her beautifully mussed hair. "I know I cannot simply buy you another to replace so special a keepsake from your mother. Jem and I think the halves can be glued together sufficiently for you to d-display it or tuck it away for safekeeping. They're clamped now and d-drying—"

She raised her head and stared at him with shining eyes. "You are the most marvelous man."

His face heated all over again. "Such p-praise."

"Well deserved."

And if they continued on this path, he'd have her frothy night rail banished to the floor and his body covering hers in seconds.

Though he was loath to put any distance between them, Daniel disengaged their arms and scooted down a foot. "Have you anything else to ask of me?"

His tone was brusque. He hoped she didn't take offense. Didn't—

"What's a munsons muffler?"

Of all the things she might have said... "Pardon?"

"Munsons muffler," she repeated as though he was *supposed* to know. "I heard it at Sarah's party when the men greeted you. The night we met."

Daniel cast about his brain. "Lord Munson? He and I sparred the d-day b-before. He got in a good punisher, a *muffler*, when he was faster than me." He shrugged. "That's the b-best I can figure."

"You really should learn how to hunker and block. Don't you have a Tremayne coat of arms? Painted on a shield you could use—?"

At the image of bringing a medieval shield into the ring, there he went, laughing again. Which was good. He had important things to say and laughing with Thea always seemed to loosen his throat.

Reluctantly, he stood. "Now p-pull on your wrapper and join me downstairs. If I have to see you in that b-bed one more minute, I'm liable to fall on you like a rabid d-dog and never get the rest out."

7

STARS & SCANDALS ~ MORE POETIC THAN HE THOUGHT

THE HOUSE WAS SETTLED and silent when Thea made her way toward the drawing room. While he'd lit a surprisingly large number of candles (judging by the glow that reached her well into the hallway), she'd tidied her appearance and done her best to suppress nervously flapping butterflies. What was so important he had to tell her in a more formal setting?

When she entered, Cyclops appeared enthralled with the scraps of beef and bone he noisily gnawed on near the banked hearth, and Daniel—

Her breath sighed out.

For when she glanced his way, Daniel stopped idly rubbing the ivory knob of his walking stick and set it aside. Standing, he waited for her to join him. So big and masculine, casually handsome, *so very appealing*, she feared her hard-won composure would soon crumble.

He'd removed his waistcoat and loosened his cravat. The ends hung loosely, exposing—

"What's that on your neck?" Shutting the door behind her, she went straight to him and peeled back his shirt. Angry red lines slashed across the curve of his shoulder, two and three at a time. She placed her fingers over the worst of the thin welts and met his gaze. "A new style of sparring?"

A rueful grin lifted his lips at both corners. "That's why Cyclops is here. We have more company at home. Feline company."

Her brow crinkled at his perplexing explanation. Feline company? What manner—

"Mrs. Freshley and her six kittens had moved in t-to your old room, t-tucked themselves nicely under that falling-over chest."

Mrs. *Freshley*? A mama cat had been in that den of despair? Which explained the soft cries she'd heard. A mama cat he'd named after her silly, child-hood poem?

The ragged skin beneath her fingers burned hot. "And you *rescued* her?"

Would this man never cease to amaze her?

"With help." His big body shifted and she let her hand glide lightly over the scratches and fall to her side.

It was impossible to be this close to him and not touch, so she moved back. He'd asked her to come downstairs to tell her something. Something serious.

Something that took precedence over joining her

in bed and finishing what his tongue had so flirta-tiously started. Best she remembered that.

Oh heavens—she tensed at the unbidden idea—was he here to tell her goodbye?

"They're ensconced in an extra bedchamber until she quits trying t-to t-take a chunk out of every-one." It took Thea a second to realize he was still talking about cats—and not giving her the heave-ho back into the streets. "I'll relocate her Royal Scratch-iness to the stab-b-*bles* once her kittens are old enough. Hopefully, she and Cy will come to an accord b-by then."

At his name, Cyclops abandoned the bone and shuffled over to deliver an impressive slobber on her slippers.

Rather bemused, totally befuddled—trying not to borrow trouble and worry over what hadn't occurred—she watched the spreading stain a second, then raised her gaze to Daniel's. The soft expression in his eyes laid her bare.

"I love you." Did that just fly from her lips?

Granted, she'd been thinking it since last night, since Mr. Taft unwittingly revealed the reasons for Daniel's ongoing reticence—in actuality, she'd thought it even before—but she shouldn't have *said* it.

He hasn't been reticent today, has he? Nay, he'd poured out his heart and she could do no less.

She took a single step toward him. "I do." A step back. Then another. Then her eyes fell to her salivated-upon slippers. How could she look at him after confessing such a thing?

Both Sarah and Susan had warned her against it. *Don't let your heart rule your head, it'll hurt more when it ends,* Susan had instructed. *And with the good ones, it* always *ends.*

But Thea couldn't avoid the truth. "Aye, I do. Love you, that is. But I shall…" And she could no longer avoid him, having to glance up as she finished, somehow the words easier to say to his startled gaze than to her spit-riddled shoes. "You're an incredible man, Daniel Tremayne, but let's forget I said that, shall we?"

"Never." The growl came just before he hauled her against him. "I'll never forget and you can nnn"—he exhaled near her ear—"*never* take it back."

"I can't?" *I don't want to.*

Still holding her tight, he whispered, "And it's Holbrook, sweet Thea. D-Daniel Anthony Holb-b-*brook*. Tremayne's just the title."

Just the title, she thought on a hysterical giggle. "Aye, well, it's a mighty imposing title and a lovely and strong name."

"It should be yours t-too."

What? Stunned, she pulled back and stared at him.

"Holb-b— Dammit, Hol…brook." Though his jaw had clenched, his eyes, his hands bracketing her waist remained tender. "You. Thea *Holbrook*, not Hurwell."

"I— I—" *I ought to be poked in the eye for even remotely thinking you mean that.* "I think you've rescued one too many strays, Lord Tremayne," she said using his title, hoping it would put some distance between them. "We've— *They*'ve marched away with your wits."

His fingers tightened and he gave her a little shake, bringing her abdomen into contact with his upper thighs. "Strays?"

"Cyclops, Buttons and John." His deaf house-keeper and who knew how many others of his staff. "Your new batch of kittens. *Me.*"

"Ah, but haven't you noticed how I *keep* any strays I care enough to bring home?" He skimmed his hands up from her waist to cup her cheeks, to stroke the sides of her face. "Thea. You...are...*not*..." In between every word, he pressed his lips to hers. "Just...a...passing...fancy...t-to...me."

After finishing that touching statement, he kissed her deeply, wielding his mouth and tongue like a weapon of sensual torment. His hands drifted to her shoulders, her back. They shaped her spine and derrière, lifted her to her toes and coiled her arms around his neck.

As the flames from his kiss licked deeper, lower, weaving throughout her body and sapping caution, her last coherent thought was: *So much for distance. I guess he truly isn't telling me goodbye.*

She grew lighthearted, light-headed at relief and lack of air, his powerful kiss stealing her breath.

Feeling him harden against her stomach, Thea moaned and arched closer.

With a ragged groan, he parted their lips. "Nay. Nnn-not yet." He swore, eased her to her feet, and then released her to step back. Putting unmistakable distance between them. Physical and otherwise.

Why?

"Sarah. Your friend," he said in a rigid tone, and Thea couldn't decipher the look on his face. "How invested is she in P-Penry?"

"Invested?" Disquiet over the feelings she'd just verbalized gave way to concern about Sarah. As she mulled the question, her fingers flew to her lips— damp and sensitive from the pressure of his mouth, it was a moment before she realized Cyclops had rested his muzzle on her slipper again.

Forcing her hand down, she curved it against her belly, hoping to quell the increased fluttering. His kiss—gracious, all of tonight—had knocked her askew. "I don't grasp your meaning."

"Sarah," he said again, jaw flexing. "I may be speaking out of t-turn, so please keep this to yourself for nn-now, but if P-P-*Penry* d-dissolves their association, will she suffer? B-be crushed? Or will she suffice?"

He gave consideration to a paid mistress? One that wasn't his own?

You, he'd said. *Thea Holbrook, not Hurwell.*

Numbness gripped Thea, disbelief still whirling about her brain. *Sarah! He's asking about your friend. Answer him.* "Um. Sarah. She'll be disappointed, of that I have no doubt. But crushed?" Her fist dug harder into her middle as she recalled what Sarah had said in the carriage: *He's paying for your services. It's naught but a business transaction.*

Her fist relaxed and she gave a quick shake of her head. "Nay. Sarah will manage. Though I know you wouldn't ask if there wasn't cause. You'll tell me, then, if you find Lord Penry means to end things? So I can prepare her?"

His sharp nod was decisive.

"Sarah knows she's naught but a paid whore, that we both—"

"Thea!" The snarl rumbled the floor beneath her feet.

"She told me 'twas so!" Thea defended, thinking how she needed the reminder, reality having set in after learning her friend's comfortable situation was likely coming to an end.

This was a temporary life she led; no doubt, she'd mistaken his words earlier.

"Thea. Wo...man!" The floor shook again as he drew out the syllables.

"You look furious."

"As well I should. I nn-never want to hear such a d-d-*derogatory term* cross your lips!" He advanced until he was inches from her face. "N-n-not ab-bout yourself or those you consider friends. D-do you hear me?"

Likely the whole neighborhood heard him.

Fully chastised by the vehemence he didn't

attempt to suppress, she nodded. "Quite. A whore nevermore," she quipped, hoping for a smile.

She was rewarded with a twitch of his lips and decided that would serve.

"But now I have more to say." He breathed deeply. Then deeper still, and she had the distinct impression he was preparing himself for battle. "Say t-to you." His words had grown raspier, the planes of his face more chiseled. "May I cont-t-tinue?"

Knowing she'd best not interrupt but let him share what he needed with as few words as possible, she nodded. "Please."

"Yester-d-day at the committee meeting, I spoke in front of p-peers. *Spoke*, to a group of men doing nothing b-but sitting and listening—or staring at the wall. I'm not sure they wanted to b-be there any more than I. But d-don't you see, I'd always thought *that* was my greatest fear."

He paused and she realized he'd just confessed something profound. "Now you know it isn't? That you fear something more?"

Eyes stark but impossibly full of emotion, he said clearly, "'T-tis the thought of losing the chance t-to love you that b-br-brings me to my knees."

That was rather telling. Or was it? Was she only hearing what she wanted to?

You. Thea Holbrook, not Hurwell.

She didn't just feel dizzy and off-balance. Nay, she felt as though she inhabited the body—the life —of a stranger. Magical things didn't happen to her. Not since she was a child and Mama wove stories about fairy princesses and far-off castles. Castles with moats and princes and—

"Thea? D-don't swoon on me now."

He shook her upper arms and her feet landed with a thump, reality coming up hard in the form of the floor. In the form of one rapidly cooling foot thanks to the slavering attentions of Cyclops.

She was mistaken. 'Tis all.

He *wasn't* asking her to marry him. Wasn't—

"Oh, but I am, sweet Thea."

He was? And she'd said that out loud?

"What of your *family*?" It came out nearly screeched and she swallowed, tempered her tone. "Lord Wylde? Lord Penry and—"

She thought he muttered something less than complimentary about Lord Penry. But then louder and clearly, he told her, "Ellie's the only close relative I claim. She's b-beyond thrilled. Has, in fact, already b-b-*begun* planning the wedding."

The *wedding*? Theirs? "Naaaaayyy..."

"Doing horse imitations now, are we?"

Thea sputtered.

"Indeed. As for Wylde, his reputation is so tarnn-nished it's practically rust. D-did you sense d-disapproval from him the other night?"

"Not exactly." Was this her? Calmly discussing *this*? As if it were possible? "But he's quite indecipherable."

"Unlike my sister, eh?" He smiled, stroked his palms from her shoulders to her elbows. "Told me you were fetching. He'll b-be fine. As to anyone else, it matters not. I've learned to live my life in ways that p-pl-*please* me and those I care for. You're part of that small, growing number now."

As his conviction and sincerity started to build, and the magical, moat-surrounded castle receded to be replaced by the truth of what this wondrous man offered, her soggy slipper ceased to matter, toes started to warm...

"I wrote you a p-poem."

"But you hate poetry."

"And I adore you. Planned on t-telling you so when I came over, even b-before your d-declaration sang past my ears."

And there it went, wet toes abounded once again, her heart melting right back into her slipper. "D-Daniel."

His thumb caressed her inner arm as he smiled. "That's my pro-nn-*nun*ciation."

Their shared laughter didn't stop her from thinking she really ought to be the voice of reason. She pulled away. "'Tis a lovely sentiment but who knows if I can conceive?" The reality of that had to be faced. Wishing wouldn't make it so. "Years with Mr. Hurwell yielded naught. And that *is* the sole purpose of a peer's wife."

He was already shaking his head. "Ah, b-but you haven't given years with *me* a chance."

"Daniel!" He was making this so difficult. "The reality is you need a titled lady. *An equal*, to bear your heir and—"

He hushed her with his lips. "What—*who*—I

nneed is you. No more blathering about equals. I'm more of a man with you than I ever was without. I trust the future will t-take care of itself—as long as ours is ent-t-twined. Now sit."

Feeling more than a bit out of sorts, she turned to Cyclops. "Do you let him talk to you that way?"

"Woof!"

"Thea."

"You growl more than your dog, do you know that?" The heated glare he sent her had her feet stumbling backward until she felt the edge of the desktop at her posterior. She hitched one side of her bottom on its surface. "There. I'm sitting. Are you sure you didn't fight someone today—other than Mrs. Freshley? Get clobbered on the head? Oh wait—you did!" *Grimmett had been that morning?*

He answered her banter seriously. "I'm d-done with fighting, Thea. I'll train Tom, maybe spar a b-bit a few times a year but no more weekly p-pummelings to prove I'm a man or p-punish myself for living when David didn't. You made me see that.

"Now I've worked on this p-poem and speech just for you. Do you want t-to hear it or not?"

"By all means. I can hardly breathe, I'm so bound with anticipation. But I can hear you going hoarse. I do believe you've talked more in the last hour than in all the time I've known you. Should you not rest? I can be patient." Oh, but 'twould surely send her out to sea.

He came up in front of her, the tendons in his

strong neck flexing as he swallowed. "It cannot wait. *I* cannot wait."

The desk beneath her backside was as hard as his whiskered jaw. She feathered her fingers over the beckoning bristle. "Daniel, what if you hurt yourself?"

"Will hurt more t-to keep quiet. Now hush and listen."

Her hand found its way to his chest, just over his hammering heart. "Rapt silence. I shall endeavor to give it to you until you ask for something else."

"Minx." He cleared his throat. Once. Twice. He backed up several paces and clasped his hands behind him. Then he began to speak with that same measured, purposeful quality she'd always found so appealing. "You asked me several questions once. I would like to answer them now.

"I spend my days thinking of you.

"Matters that concern me include fixing that damn orrery—which is finally done, thanks to you and my meddling sister. Getting a good night's sleep. Seeing Ellie made happy. And now you as well..."

As he spoke, answering all the items Thea had listed in that audacious letter, she realized she no longer noticed the stammer. The sound of his deep, so desired, voice glided past her ears without hesitation and went straight to her heart.

She grabbed the sharp edge of the desk and held on. Because with every word this man uttered, he swept her feet right out from under her.

"What do I like? How you viewed me as a whole

man before I did myself. I was lost before you, Thea, like a little boy. But through you, I found my way home.

"Gads, I like so much about you—your patience, your smile. How you laugh at the absurd and have taught me to do the same.

"I adore your beautifully expressive eyes, how gentle and caring they are at times, brimming with inner fire at others. How they recall to mind things best recalled and have returned to me sweet memories of the past I'd forgotten before you came into my life.

"I love how you look at me when I talk to you, how calmly you wait, without ever hurrying me to rush my words.

"I love how you ask me to do naughty things to your bum and blush while saying it." (Which only made her face flame anew.)

"How you've opened my eyes—and lugs—to the pleasures to be found beyond my study.

"I could go on, and I will—another time."

She nodded when he paused, seemingly for her agreement. How much more could she take? Her heart was full to bursting.

"I dream of you. Have, I think, for a long while now, but it took meeting you to make me realize all I've been missing." Fearful of fainting on him, given all he now shared, she scooted back until she sat squarely on the desk, feet dangling, fingers still gripping the edge.

"And I had a devil of a time making this part out,

but no, I'm definitely not married and have no children. Save for the ones I pray you'll give me. Or let me give you?" He winked. "It's a task I'm willing to work on with the utmost of diligence."

Thea's loins sweltered at that. Dazed, she tried to nod but only succeeded in wobbling in place.

"I've written you a poem."

The solemn way he spoke, the look in his eyes— and the fact that he'd mentioned it thrice now—told her that, clearly, this seemingly simple event was of no little significance. "Well then..." She unpried her fingers from the desk and extended her hand. "I'd be delighted to read it."

"Nay. Poetry is meant to be recited aloud." He paced forward until poised confidently at her knees. With broad hands to each, he widened them and stepped directly between. His face was stern but his eyes, they sparkled at her.

"Roses are red, my name is Daniel. Come be with me. Let's create a scandal."

"A scandal?" she whispered, flustered.

He jerked a nod, licked his lips and very deliberately said, "Now I *am* asking for something else, other than your silence, so feel at liberty to chatter away."

"What?" The question was a near silent sigh.

"Your hand. Your trust. Your life, meshed with mine. I'm asking you to marry me, Thea."

He really meant it! "And live merrily married forevermore?"

"Aye. Though you make light, I do not. 'Tis

serious business, woman, talk of taking a mate. A willing leg shackle. Marry me, Thea," he coaxed, digging his thumbs into the tender flesh above her knees. "Love me. Mother my children."

She opened her mouth to protest again but he overrode her before a single sound emerged. "Before you worry overmuch, know that if we don't have our own, England is bursting with babes in need of loving homes."

"More strays?"

"More love."

A whirlwind of feeling pressed behind her rapidly blinking eyelids. She willed it to recede.

"*Family*, Thea." He said it with such strength, such convincing sincerity. "Ours. If you would but agree."

"I..." She gulped. Could she really do that to him? Condemn him and Lady Elizabeth to be ostracized, cast from the social strata that was their birthright? Just because he offered her the world?

For that's what marriage to a peer was—an impossible dream akin to a trip to the moon. *He loves you, Dorothea Jane. Loves you.* "I..."

"Thea," he leaned forward to breathe in her ear. "You're wavering. I can tell."

He pulled back to catch her gaze. "I know it's incredibly sudden, but I love you to the stars and beyond, and I need you to say yes. I need *you*."

The moon *and* the stars?

He hadn't just promised her the known world but the entire universe.

Her toes curled in slippers that suddenly went from damp to snuggly warm. She released her hold on the desk to loop her arms around his neck. "I will."

"Will...?"

"Marry you!" Thea catapulted off her precarious perch and into the haven of his arms. "Always! Always, you wonderful, marvelous man. It was the stars that did it. I rather fancy being loved to them."

"Not the deuced poem?" Though he tried for cranky, she could tell by the way he hugged her how very pleased she'd made him.

"That too." Then she was kissing him and he her, laughing and—

Thea sniffed.

Then sniffed again.

"Oh, look..." She blinked horridly fast and ran her sleeve across her nose. "You've turned me into a snoaching sniveler."

"And you've turned me into a wretched poet. Fine pair we make."

"Fine pair indeed."

The End

Thanks for reading *DARING DECLARATIONS*. I adored Daniel and Thea from the moment I met them; I hope you did too. :)

These two characters have lived on in my heart more than others who have found their happily-ever-after. Like Daniel, I sometimes have trouble speaking, only from a musculature standpoint not because of severe stuttering, and for an author who uses dictation software to write, that's frustrating on so many levels. I think I may relate to him more than other characters (so much more, that I think I've developed a crush—shhh! We'll not tell Thea or Mr. Lyons about that, all right?).

If you have a chance to write a review, it's always appreciated. Reviews and word-of-mouth are two of the best things you can do for authors you enjoy.

Meanwhile, take peace in the quiet moments and speak up when you need to. ;)

What's Next?

WHOO-HOO! I'm glad you wondered, because I am thrilled to report that my Roaring Rogue Regency Shapeshifters are back! With book one, *Ensnared by Innocence*, available now!

I immersed myself in rewrites (escaping to 1812 for some much-appreciated peace of mind!), fleshing out the story from its original publication and sparking the language to better sound Regency-esque. :)

ENSNARED BY INNOCENCE...

Changing into a lion isn't all fur and games.

Turn or swipe the page for the blurb and first chapter, and get ready for some roaring fun times.

Ensnared by Innocence

A Regency lord battles his inner beast while helping an innocent miss, never dreaming how he'll come to care for the chit—nor how being near his world will deliver danger right to her doorstep.

If Darcy had been a shape-shifting lion who thought about frisking—a lot...

Lady Francine Montfort may have led a sheltered life till her parents' untimely demise but that doesn't mean she's ignorant. Neither is she blind to the conniving ways of her persistent aunt, who's determined to marry Francine off for her own selfish gain. Forced to drastic measures to avoid the wretched woman's scheming, Francine concocts her own masterful plan.

She might need to beg a favor from Lord Blakely —the sinfully alluring marquis who inspires all manner of illicit thoughts—but she's determined to help him as well. To ease those mysterious, haunting secrets that torment him so...

When Lady Francine, the epitome of innocence, requests he pose as her betrothed, Blakely knows he should handily refuse. He's baffled when unfamiliar, protective urges make themselves known, tempting him to agree while danger stalks ever closer.

Alas, it's fast approaching the season when Blakely loses all control. Either Francine satisfies his sexual appetites or he'll be forced to reveal his beastly side. And that will never do. Not now that he's come to care for the intrepid miss.

STANDALONE ~ HEA ~ 80,000-WORD NOVEL ~ BOOK 1 - ROARING ROGUES REGENCY SHIFTERS

Note: This love story between two people contains some profanity and a lot of sizzle, including one partial ménage scene that gets rather...growly.

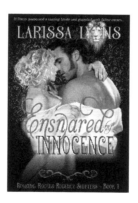

Chapter 1
The Preposterous Proposition

────────◗○◖────────

I leave this recordation for my beloved sons. Erasmus and Nash. My heirs. Who will one day, pray God, live to manhood and conduct themselves in a manner more gracious, more fitting to their station and responsibilities than I have managed.

My dear offspring who I cannot believe I condemned to such a fate, however unknowingly.

A fate I share but one that was not known to me until after you were both conceived. (And which also no doubt explains the sparsity of children in our family, and siblings for you both.)

The urges for The Change first came upon me in the summer of the year I turned five and twenty. It was not yet the middle of July and yet I sensed the stirrings of what I would eventually learn was my animal blood. My feline side, if you boys will only set aside skepticism and believe. Please, sons, heed my warnings, for you do not want to be caught unaware as I—and irreparably harm the woman you love.

To see the fear in her eyes when she looks upon you and beholds a monster. A beast. Your inner beast. The lion, untamable. Unstoppable.

Deadly?

I pray not. 'Tis why I locked myself away, in this, my 28th year, the third of the curse. Why I place armed guards at the door for the entirety of the month.

As I battle the inner demon once again, my only consolation is knowing that you both are still too young to remark upon my absence.

Too young to question why Papa turns into an ogre toward the end of the hot, sultry summer months.

Too young to recall how severely I injured your mother...

LONDON, ENGLAND
MAY 1812

"Lord Blakely, pardon the interruption. Might I beg a word with you?"

Erasmus Hammond, Marquis of Blakely, looked down his long patrician—scarred—nose at the intrepid female who dared interrupt the boisterous group of men he currently conversed with.

Delicate, feminine young ladies such as this one definitely did *not* mix with his oft-beastly ways. Not unless they wanted to be torn asunder.

He didn't recognize her, but judging from the looks his companions aimed her direction, they did. The meaning behind the smirks and elbow jabs was unmistakable, confound it.

Just what he didn't need—another wedding-minded miss setting her cap for him. Every Season he remained unmarried, it seemed his value on the marriage market escalated. Despite the air of libidinous rake he cultivated in public—and indulged in private—his attraction as an eligible mate only increased with each year that passed, as though snaring his dissolute self would be something of a coup. Hardly.

Where was her chaperone?

"Gracious me," he drawled as sarcastically as he could manage, "a bold little muff, are you not?" He gestured to his chortling companions, hoping the crude comment would be enough to send her heels flying. "Approaching *me*? Here?"

Here, at Lady Longford's crush, celebrating the engagement of one of her many offspring, the place teeming with too many people and too much perspiration, offensive odors he chronicled as easily as breathing. Odors he tolerated, along with the boorish twaddle that surrounded him, because unlike some others he could name—ahem, his brother for one—Blakely bore his responsibilities, took them very seriously indeed.

Yet, no sweat-drenched, unpalatable odors emanated from the brash one before him, he couldn't help but note. So she wasn't here to dance and make merry?

Dance and make a marriage, more like. Is that not the ultimate aim of every young chit here?

Blakely grunted at the thought, taking her in.

The very definition of English miss—blonde, blue-eyed and insipid—stood before him. Granted, she was a trifle taller than perfection allowed these days, and her face looked decidedly powdered—smelled powdered too, the pale artifice likely hiding all manner of spots, blemishes and daunting imperfections.

But when she shifted, allowing the shawl curved within the crooks of both arms to slide, he noticed the two-inch expanse of skin between the short, puffy sleeves of her gown and her long gloves. Two inches of implausibly dark skin, which forced his attention back to her face. Caused him to study...to linger. Beneath the powder, 'twas smooth as silk. At least that's how it appeared, making his fingers twitch with the sudden urge to test the observation.

So she wasn't hiding spots? Perchance only an unfashionable liking of the sun? As one who spent more time than he'd like in the dark, that alone piqued his interest.

"Please, my lord?" She scooted further around the column separating his small group from the dance floor. "I promise not to take but a few moments of your time." So earnest. Her voice so very serene, even as he scented her... What was it? Fear? Frustration? Apprehension that her asinine errand —approaching him, of all people—would prove unsuccessful?

Of course it would. It has to.

Trying again to discourage her, he glanced around the ballroom, purposely avoiding her gaze and employed his loftiest voice. "I do not believe we have been introduced and therefore, most regretfully, I cannot begin any manner of discourse with—"

"But we have," she had the audacity to interject. "It was three years ago at the Seftons' ball. We danced, but I have no expectation that you recollect the encounter."

He didn't.

And he knew she was shamming him. If they'd met, if he'd been near her for a dance, he'd remember her scent.

A remarkably fresh yet earthy fragrance that

appealed to him on so many levels 'twas dangerous. Dangerous for them both.

She stood her ground and spoke calmly, despite their eavesdropping, snickering audience. Taller than most women, she came nearly to his chin. Hers was tilted at such an angle he suspected she must practice the determined stance in front of a mirror.

More than that, most fresh-faced elegants weren't bold enough to approach him directly, and he couldn't help but admire this one in spite of himself. He almost hated to crush her spirit but dissuade her he must. Innocents were not for him. Especially now.

It was nearing the time of year he had two choices: Either secret himself away and privately battle his demons. Or find the wildest women he could to exorcise away his fiendish tendencies through exhaustive, nightly rounds of intense prigging. Smashing choice, that. No wonder he always chose the second, more sociable option. Something he seriously doubted would appeal to this one.

"By all means, do forgive me," he stated, matching her tranquil tone. "But, alas, you are correct. I do not remember you." There was more jostling from his cohorts. They knew the type of female he preferred—and the kind he avoided at all costs. Though several years beyond the schoolroom, the flaxen-haired miss in front of him definitely fell into the latter category.

Even so, he was surprised how her poise drew him. And if he tipped his head...just so...

Ah, yes, he *could* look straight down the front of her pale blue gown, to furtively gaze at the womanly endowments not quite hidden beneath. Of course, he had no business looking at her dugs, none whatsoever.

"A *word*?" she insisted, angling her chin a fraction higher. "Consider it imperative."

Imperative? Intrigued despite his better judgment, he inclined his head in a show of assent.

'Twas odd, how her voice drew him, all calm assurance instead of the more heated, sultry tones he was used to hearing from his experienced lovers. Would she maintain that cultured, confident manner in the throes of passion?

What of it, man? She's not for you.

True. So very true.

Especially now, with his latest suspicions? With even more danger surrounding London than before...

Had he missed one? Failed to pick up on a potential wrong-side-of-the-blanket Hammond offspring? Had all the sacrifices, the years spent miring himself in the dungeons of the *ton*, seeking out the most dissolute, reckless individuals, praying they were only human—and nothing more sinister—been all for naught?

Shaking off the dread that accompanied him these days like a persistent and bothersome fly, he followed her a short distance further, away from the periphery of the crowded dance floor.

When she reached a secluded corner and

stopped, he did as well. And found himself curious, if only remotely so, why she had approached *him* directly—and without a formal introduction. Totally unheard of in the upper realms of the *ton* he inhabited.

"Lord Blakely, I have a proposition I would like to put forth to you." For all her height and assured poise, she seemed dainty, almost fragile, standing before him.

"By all means, please do." His curiosity grew by the second. And so did the reluctant attraction running rampant through his veins. Which would never do.

Never! Do you not have sufficient responsibilities, man? Ferreting out who's destroying—

Blakely shook off the annoying reminder, the one that settled fear and concern heavily on his shoulders; far more pleasant to ponder the diverting package before him. "State your case," he encouraged in as droll a voice as he could cultivate, "so I may rejoin my crew."

When she hesitated, glancing behind her, he took possession of the gloved hand nearest—which brought her attention swiftly back to him. He then lifted it to his lips and kissed the air over her fingers before releasing them. Instead of scaring her away as he'd intended, a blush flared up her chest and over her face, delighting him, which was patently ridiculous.

Blushes were for maidens; whores were for him.

So why was it that the tinge of pink flushing her

cheeks fascinated? The slight color was difficult to discern beneath the powder and her unfashionably dark skin but he saw it clearly nevertheless. Unbidden, curiosity rose regarding the extent of her exposure to sunlight. Where might the golden hue leave off and pale porcelain begin?

And why do you care?

Aye, definitely time to curtail their conversation. "You were saying? A proposition, I believe. I weary of being here," he lied. "Speak in haste."

The pale blonde ringlets surrounding her face swayed as she took a fortifying breath, readying for battle. "I know I presume much, but I would be eternally grateful if you could see your way to posing as my betrothed until—"

He laughed outright at her outrageous request, drawing the attention of several guests. Sobering, Blakely stated, "Completely out of the question. But thank you for asking. I needed some amusement this evening."

When he turned to leave, her hand shot out, latching on to his arm with surprising strength. He halted and peered at her gloved fingers until she removed them. Damn if a bolt of *need* hadn't flashed through him at the contact. Astonishing, for he'd just dallied with the amorous and very accommodating Mistress Rose of the Crown & Cock not twenty-four hours before.

"Lord Blakely, please. Hear me out." She rushed on before he could say yea or nay. "It would be a pretend betrothal, a farce if you will, lasting only a few weeks. Surely you can find it in your heart to assist me for such a short time? I will pay you handsomely for your trouble and release you publicly from our agreed-upon understanding after you fulfill its terms."

"We have no understanding," he felt compelled to remind her. "But for the sake of argument, your reasoning is faulty. How would this assist you in any way? For upon becoming affianced to me, not to mention later breaking said betrothal, your reputation would be tantamount to ruined."

"That has no consequence," she said rather convincingly. "I only want the *appearance* of a betrothal for the remainder of the Season."

Which only intrigued him further. What manner of eligible miss cared naught for her reputation? 'Twas a young female's only currency, all her real blunt controlled first by her father and then by her spouse. "And why is that?"

"My reasons are my own."

Stubborn chit. He half wished he couldn't see her so clearly in the candlelit ballroom. What was it about her that drew him?

The unspoilt scent of heather and fresh air? The sunshine she exudes? The hint of freedom from the chains that bind you to London as surely as if you were locked in Newgate.

"If you will not explain yourself, why should I even consider your ridiculous proposal?"

That willful chin lifted again. "Because I will pay you."

"Not enough, not for what you ask." She had no *idea* what she was asking, what being near her the next few weeks might cost him. Or her.

She proceeded to name an amount that sent his head spinning.

Good God. He'd just been propositioned by a bloody heiress.

To fight the deceptive allure she represented—because it wasn't called a *leg shackle* for nothing—he shifted his weight, tightened the muscles in his legs. "You are a piece of intriguing baggage, I'll grant you that. Why approach me and not some other titled gent in need of the ready and likely to agree?"

"Your standing as one of the most sought-after libertines in the *ton*," she stated baldly, her face flushing even more. "It suits my purposes quite well. And your title, for another reason. Not every marquis has a character such as yours."

"I do not know whether to be insulted or flattered." The inexplicable urge to touch her cheek stormed through him. Since when did he care about cheeks? He fisted his hands and anchored them firmly at his sides.

"I mean no offense, I assure you, but it is not in me to cavil at the truth. You and I both know that you have no intention of marrying this year, and I need someone of your...*ilk* to best ensure the successful outcome of my plan."

He made a noise in his throat, one that could indicate he was considering her asinine idea, which was absurd—because he wasn't. Neither was he convinced he wanted his *ilk*—well-suited to her asinine plan or not—to be what he was known for. Sought after for.

"I only ask that you show me the same courtesy and give me your honest reply posthaste." Again, she looked over her shoulder, as if expecting a dragon to swoop in and steal her away.

Come to think on it, he was surprised they had been left alone this long. "And what is your next course of action, should I turn down your oh-so-tempting offer?"

"Sarcasm does not become you, Lord Blakely," she admonished him.

"Do not talk down to me," he told her, instantly irritated with himself. With her. Why was he still wasting his breath conversing? Why not simply tell her nay and be done with it? Why did he long to touch so much more than her cheek? To see her hair down, her dress gone and her legs wrapped around his waist?

Damn it, where was his control? It seemed to have abandoned him the very moment *she* abandoned her good sense and approached him.

"Forgive me," she said contritely. "The stress of awaiting your reply has put me quite on edge."

"Which is understandable. Considering you have propositioned a man who has not the faintest clue who you are."

"Lady Francine Montfort, my lord." She sketched the briefest curtsy on record.

"Please continue, Lady Francine Montfort." He

committed her name to memory; her scent he'd never forget—even if he tried. "When I refuse to be a part of your outlandish scheme, what will you do?"

"*When* you refuse?" She arched a single, chastising eyebrow.

How the hell an eyebrow lift could make him feel small only strengthened his resolve. *Say nay and be gone!*

"If you persist in claiming you have already decided"—she gave a prim little huff—"then there remains no further need to waste your time. Or mine. Good night."

This time it was his hand that halted her retreat.

She spun silently on slippered feet back to him. "Yes, my lord?" Her tone had turned icy.

Blakely released her at once, the tingles attacking his palm something of a surprise. "Humor me, then. *If*. If I decline. What is your plan?"

"Why, I will speak with the next person on my list. Perhaps *he* will be more agreeable."

Unaccountably, disappointment stirred in his chest. "Oh? So this is not an exclusive offer you make to me alone? I am only one in a long line?" *And no doubt farther down the list than your pride deems acceptable.* "Lady Francine Montfort," he continued, and it was an effort to maintain his droll façade, "I must confess I am crushed by the knowledge. Quite."

She looked over her shoulder again, distracted by whatever it was she sought. "If you must know…" Her gaze swung back to his. "You are my preferred choice and the first man I approached, but as you are determined to thwart my sincere overtures, I must move on. I beg of you, please do not speak of this to anyone. It—"

"I would not dream of it."

"Are you positive I cannot persuade you to at least consider my proposition? You have yet to hear my terms in their entirety and yet you are refusing me outright."

"There is more?" The entreaty in her sky-blue eyes was almost enough to convince him to reconsider. But then he saw past the appeal, to the innocence.

Pity. He didn't deal with innocents. Ever. Only those women already hardened by life's experiences, women who liked having their precious egos petted as much as they liked having their slits stroked. Women whose purses he was not averse to lining and who were willing to overlook his behavior, if, in the midst of things, he got a little rough. Certainly, his carnal appetites were too wild for the virtuous dainty before him.

Somewhat regretfully, he opened his mouth to decline.

"Frannnny!"

The screech interrupted him.

"How *dare* you!" An older woman charged at them from the side, brandishing her fan like a bayonet and casting him a glare as if he were Lucifer come to life. Which perhaps he was—for even considering corrupting her charge.

"Franny! You *evil* child!" Sky-high plum-colored

feathers stuck out of a forest-green turban, agitating the air above her mottled face. Ire definitely did not sit pretty on this particular matron. "What *are* you doing, talking to *him*?" the woman hissed. Her voice carried like that of a general commanding his troops. More than one curious head turned toward their secluded corner. "Come away this instant!"

"But, Aunt," Lady Francine protested, casting him a commiserating glance. "Lord Blakely and I are only conver—"

"The Lord Blakelys of this world are most certainly *not* for the likes of you, gel. Now come along." A full head shorter and three times as wide as her niece, the harridan grasped Lady Francine's slim arm and tugged.

Pale-blue eyes gazed at him as she silently succumbed to the forced retreat. Just before she disappeared from view, her mouth formed the words, *The garden?*

And he, purveyor of pleasure and avoider of innocents, found himself nodding in assent.

Damn his hide.

Ensnared by Innocence - Read it today!

ABOUT LARISSA
HUMOR. HEARTFELT EMOTION. & HUNKS.

A lifelong Texan, Larissa writes sexy contemporaries and steamy regencies, blending heartfelt emotion with doses of laugh-out-loud humor. Her heroes are strong men with a weakness for the right woman.

Avoiding housework one word at a time (thanks in part to her super-helpful herd of cats >^..^<), Larissa adores brownies, James Bond, and her husband. She's been a clown, a tax analyst, and a pig castrator(!) but nothing satisfies quite like seeing the entertaining voices in her head come to life on the page.

Writing around some health challenges and computer limitations, it's a while between releases, but stick with her...she's working on the next one.

Learn more at LarissaLyons.com.

- amazon.com/author/larissalyons
- bookbub.com/authors/larissa-lyons
- goodreads.com/larissalyons
- facebook.com/AuthorLarissaLyons
- instagram.com/larissa_lyons_author

Printed in Great Britain
by Amazon